Beautiful
Things
Never
Last

A novel

STEPH CAMPBELL

Beautiful Things Never Last

Copyright © 2013 by Steph Campbell

All rights reserved. Printed in the United States of America.

No part of this book may be used or reproduced in any form or by any means electronic or mechanical, including photocopying, recording, or by any information storage and retrieval systems, without prior written permission of the author except where permitted by law.

Published by
Steph Campbell

Cover photo by: Darla Winn
Cover design by: Sarah Hansen at Okay Creations.

The characters and events portrayed in this book are fictitious. Any similarity to real persons, living or dead is coincidental and not intended by the author.

For my Dad, Steve.

And the rest of the DiBella family— for sharing your love, the best food on the planet, and the truth that family doesn't always mean blood.

Love you all.

(*Now* can I have the sauce recipe?)

*Renee—
Wishing you beautiful moments, beautiful friendships & beautiful loves that last.
xx—
Jayne Allen*

Beautiful Things Never Last

is a love letter to those that are brave enough to give second chances, accept that sometimes love is messy and hard—even when it's good,

and those that can open their hearts wide enough to allow forgiveness in.

One

BEN

My cell phone acts as a piss-poor light in the pitch black apartment but it'll have to do, because I don't want to risk waking Quinn. I lock the front door behind me, then turn and nearly trip over the damn couch, cussing myself through my teeth for not making it home until late.

Again.

It's become an all-too regular thing, me coming home late, or sneaking back out after Quinn has gone to bed. It's not like I'm running around on her, I'd never— I fucking love that woman with everything in me. But I was driving home and there was this perfect light over the water and I had to pull off of PCH and take some photos while I had the chance. I miss out on some of the best light of the day while I'm either at school or in the studio at work, so it's almost torture to not pull over and capture a little bit of that particular perfect light when I'm lucky enough to catch it. It was one of the main reasons we chose Southern California rather one of the other art schools in New York or Seattle. We wanted to be near the Pacific Ocean. I just happen to love taking advantage of our surroundings.

I slide out of my pants, pull my t-shirt over my head, and toss them both over the back of the flimsy IKEA desk chair before I push through our bedroom door.

I shine the light of my phone in the direction of the bed I share with Quinn, and can just make out her small frame, curled up with her back toward me. And it's seeing her there, peaceful but alone, that really makes me start to feel like a bastard for not being here to kiss her goodnight.

I pad across the room to our bed and slip under the blankets next to Quinn. The sight of her was one thing, but being next to her... I'm completely unable to resist pulling her a little closer to me. Her skin is warm under the heavy quilt, even though it's nearly bare. I know I shouldn't, I know it's completely counterproductive to my stealth-like entrance, but I run my hand along the band of her panties, and hook my thumb under the thin lace at her hip.

Quinn breathes in deeply and I know I've woken her up.

"Shhh..." I say. "Sorry to wake you. Go back to sleep."

She blinks several times before turning over toward me.

"It's okay." Her voice is raspy and full of sleep. Quinn snuggles into my chest and gets comfortable again. I let my eyes close as I run my hand through her long, brown hair, breathing in the familiar smell of her. "Wait, did you just get in?" The sleepiness in her voice fades quickly like a flame blown out.

"Mmm hmm," I say.

"What time is it?" Her voice has already shed all the creakiness of deep sleep and is blade sharp.

I'm not sure how to make my answer sound like anything other than a confession. It's not one. So why does it feel like it is? "Around one."

"Oh." She pauses for a few beats, and I'm not sure if she's moving her body away from my hands to make a point or because she's just trying to burrow back into a comfortable position. "Taking pictures again?"

I nod and let her wiggle out of my arms, keeping the tips of my fingers hovered over the bony curve of her hip. "I missed you."

"I cooked. I mean, yeah, of course I cooked. There's leftover manicotti in the fridge. But I wanted to talk to you. I guess it can wait until the morning. Later. Whatever. Good night." She rolls back over and pulls the quilt tight under her chin. My fingers slide along her back and into the dip of her spine, then bounce off the mattress when she tenses her back just enough to break contact.

Shit.

"Quinn." I swallow around the words, my fingers still tensed and ready, maybe, to reach for her again. If she wants. If she wants me. "I'm so sorry. I know I've been doing this a lot lately. I don't mean to be a dick, I swear."

"It's fine, I get the whole 'tortured artist' thing and that when the inspiration strikes, you have to follow it. *I do*. I just...I just miss you."

She won't look at me, because I know this type of honesty is hard for her. And I love this woman so damn much right now. I reach over her to switch on the light on the nightstand, loving the way she groans and throws her arm over her eyes, before I pull her over, flat on her back so I can really look at her, blinking like crazy, her lashes pressed together against the bright light.

"I miss you too. I'm sorry." I try to word what I'm thinking in a way that won't leave me sounding like a total putz. "I keep thinking that if I take the perfect photo, that I'll be able to sell it—"

"Ben, you could sell any one of your photos right now—today. They're amazing." She lets her eyes slit a tiny bit wider and brushes her thumb over my bottom lip, and I'm instantly filled with a total shock of the purest kind of happiness, the kind only Quinn can seem to bring to life.

I appreciate her faith in me, and my pictures are good, but not good enough for someone to pay for or to want to hang in their home. In Quinn's mind, I'm the next Andreas Gursky, which I guess is fair, since in mine, she's the next Giada De Laurentiis. But I ignore her attempt at flattering me and continue. "Did I tell you about that guy from school? He took a photograph of a rock, a rock! And sold the thing for six-figures. I keep thinking if I take the perfect photo, that I'll be able to sell it and take care of you the way you deserve."

Quinn and I are happy here. Our apartment is small, but there's only the two of us, and we're together and that's what matters. But even though we both work, it's only scraping by on our meager checks and our extra student loan money. Quinn's home life may never have been perfect, but she always had nice things, and I want to give that same security to her. I have to.

She scoffs. "You, Benjamin Shaw, are more than I ever deserved."

I kiss the part of her bottom lip where it meets her chin—my favorite place. I find a new favorite spot of her every day.

"Anyway, what do you want to talk about?" I push up the cotton top she's wearing and run my hand over the smooth skin of her stomach before pressing my lips to the same place.

She slides closer in my arms, works her hands into loose fists and runs them up and down my back. I can feel the jagged patches of half-gone nail polish. She always picks it off when she's nervous. "I have this opportunity," she finally says. "To go away for school."

"Rad, where to? For how long?" I reach over and turn on the second bedside lamp, because this is amazing news, and I want to see her when she delivers it and let her see me. I want us both awake and bathed in light when we share this to make up for all the creeping in the dark I've had to do lately.

"Italy." Quinn raises her dark eyebrows and gives me a

nervous smile that ends with her chewing the side of her lip.

"For how long?" I repeat, pretty much refusing to acknowledge that Italy is across the damn world. I don't even do well with Quinn being across the mattress. I rub my hand along her shoulder, trying to work out the tension knots that have bowed her shoulders in.

Quinn opens her eyes wide and turns the corners of her mouth up like I'm a little kid and she has to deliver some bad news as gently as she can. "Just a month."

I let out a long breath I never realized I had trapped in my lungs. "Wow. A month? Wow." I switch to rubbing my own neck, instantly tense.

It's not that I can't be without Quinn, I can. I just don't really *want* to be. It's taken a long time to get to this place we're in and I'm freaking happy as hell. But this is school…

"So, you're gonna go, right?" I ask, not about to let her see that I'm even one percent nervous about this.

This time the wide eyes and big smile are real, and her face is alive with an excitement I love. An excitement that I used to see more before things got to be such a grind in general. I didn't realize how much I missed that face until I saw it glowing in the golden light of our room. "What do you think? I mean, it's *Italy*. I'd get to see places that I'd probably never get to go on my own."

I could take you, I want to say. But I swallow the words, because right now, I can't, and who the hell knows how long it'll be before I'm able to give her what I want to. What she deserves right now. What she needs to go after.

"They had someone back out, so it's not even like I was first choice, but it's only for a handful of students. I'd get to go and learn from these chefs that are just, wow, world class, you know? It's in this amazing little town that's way off the beaten path and I can't pass it up, right?" she says, every word laced with excitement that's undeniable. It's not a question.

"Right." I say it in a way that hopefully sounds sure and confident and convincing, like I have zero doubt that this is exactly what she should be doing. But I hear the word come out sounding twisted and gruff, and anything but the right way.

Her smile flickers, but she gets a hold on it. "Okay. So, I leave on Tuesday."

All my attempts at keeping a game face are ripped out by the roots by that one word.

Tuesday?

A handful of days away?

Tuesday?

"Tuesday? Like, next week Tuesday? Why are you just now telling me this?"

Quinn and I have had a rocky road to get to where we are now, and we don't have secrets, or apparently, we do. I thought we were doing great on the communication front. Is this because I'm gone so much? I want to ask her, but I'm nervous about the answer. What the hell is going to happen if things are weird now with me just staying out too late, with her being gone for a month? I can't ask her to stay —that would make it so much worse.

Quinn shrugs, a quick rise and dip of her already knotted shoulders, and her mouth flattens into a tense line. "I don't know. I didn't find out until two weeks ago…and then, with Thanksgiving this week…and everything…I just wanted us to have a nice holiday."

It all melts for me then. She wanted us to have a nice holiday. Our first together. "And you were worried about the confrontation?"

"Maybe," she admits, her scowl losing some of its punch because of the confused squint of her eyes.

"I want you to go, baby. *I do.* I'm going to miss you something fierce. But, I'll be right here when you get back. Waiting for you to cook me dinner," I joke in a hoarse voice, because it's all I can do, and she falls into my lap and winds herself around me.

I run my hand up her thigh and watch her skin cover with goose-bumps and her nipples perk up under the tissue-paper-thin t-shirt she's wearing. I'm instantly hard. I may be used to seeing Quinn's body, but I can't help the reaction I always have to her.

"A month, huh? You'll miss Christmas." It's a little

embarrassing how much I was looking forward to Christmas with her. Last Christmas she'd shown up on my porch like a drowned rat, gorgeous and ready to make everything we'd fucked up so badly perfect again. That day changed my life, and I was all about celebrating the anniversary of that.

"That's another reason I was nervous to tell you. I mean, I wasn't going to go home to Georgia with Carter and Shayna anyway—" She picks off a fleck of glittery pink nail polish and flicks it off the side of the bed, pinching her lips together.

"It could've been just you and me here," I say, my voice low around the disappointment I can't hide. I totally get that she needs to go, but the alternative would be pretty fucking awesome, too.

"I know." Her gaze shifts down to her chipped nail polish. "I did think about that. I did. I feel like a huge jerk—"

"Quinn," I reach over and tip her chin up so that she's looking at me again, her pupils big and black in the dim light. "I want you to go. I honestly do. I'm going to miss you, but I'm proud of you. You need to do this. It is sort of weird that you'll be gone for Christmas, though. I mean, why not hold the classes in January?"

Quinn shrugs, "It is, right? The curriculum is all about traditional Italian cuisine, and leads up to the final at the end where we cook the Feast of Seven Fishes."

I smile and nod like I have any clue what she's talking about.

"Maybe...maybe you could go and see your family for Christmas?" she says it slowly, gauging my reaction as she releases each word.

I grit my teeth.

I talk to my dad semi-regularly, but I haven't talked to my mom in almost a year. It wasn't an easy pill to swallow— my deciding to pass up going to school at Columbia to instead, move to California with Quinn and go to art school. Mom probably could have gotten over my choice to pursue a career in photography, but that, combined with the choice to pursue a future with Quinn was too much for her. I know Quinn feels guilty about the lack of relationship I have with my family, but it's not her fault. I try to make her see that every chance I can. I chose her, and my mom needs to stop acting like a damn child and accept it. If she can't, I'm totally happy here.

"Maybe." I leave it vague. "Can we just concentrate on us right now? I've only got you till Tuesday."

"Ready to show me how much you'll miss me?" Quinn stares up at me and then winks.

"You're about to have your mind blown with the display of just how much I'm going to miss you." My hands tighten on her hips and my breath catches.

She smirks. "Is that a fact?"

"Ready?"

I slide the oversized t-shirt off of her shoulder and press

my mouth onto the perfect patch of now-exposed skin. I love this look on Quinn the most. Sleepy and casual and so devastatingly beautiful that I want to taste every inch of her. I want to capture this moment right here. My hand twitches at my side, wanting to grab my camera back off of the nightstand.

"No chance you're going to let me take a picture of you right now, huh?" I ask, half-hopeful, but already knowing the answer.

"No, not gonna happen," Quinn laughs and slides out from underneath me.

I lay back and she straddles her legs around me and leans in. She lets her lips hover above mine, just close enough so that her bottom lip barely brushes against my top lip when she speaks. "Thank you. For letting me do this, I mean."

"I'm not *letting* you do anything." I pull the hair back away from her face and kiss her cheeks, her nose, and her neck. "I think it's fantastic that you have this opportunity. Really."

"So, that means you're fine with it?" Her lips nuzzle my neck and her tongue flicks over my jugular, beating like crazy. She knows I can't be anything but fine when she's doing this kind of craziness to me.

"I mean, yeah, it makes me nervous. I won't be there to look out for you," I say, trying to wrangle my voice.

"Ben," she laughs, "I don't need you to take care of me."

The words are like a kick to the gut and she knows it instantly because she closes her eyes and shakes her head like she can't believe what she just said.

She grabs both hands behind her neck and blows out a long breath. "That's not what I meant…I mean, I just…fuck…I'm sorry."

I pull my lips into a tight line and nod, pulling her close to me again, but the spell's been broken. Completely broken. "Quinn, I know what you meant."

But the trouble is, I don't.

I *want* her to need me.

~~~~~~~~~~~~~~~~~

"Quinn, seriously, stop," I say. I slide my arms around her and pull the pan out of the oven.

"I got it," she says. And I know, like the weight of everything else, she can handle the weight of taking a turkey out of the oven, but still, I try to help.

She lets out an exasperated breath, blowing her long bangs out of her face. I set the bird onto the countertop and she wipes her hands on her apron, looking uncharacteristically prim and proper. *Looking* the part of the girl my mom always thought I should end up with.

"And anyway, I don't know why I'm going to all of this trouble, since it's just us." She tightens the tie on her apron and marches across the black and white linoleum floor like a woman on a mission.

"So what if it's just us?" I say. I pull the oven mitts off and cross the room to her where she's piping icing onto a chocolate pie. I nuzzle my face into her neck and breathe in the familiar smell of her.

"Sooo... You know, Thanksgiving is a *family* holiday," she says. She gives a small shrug, just that same quick jerk of her shoulders that she rolls out when she's most stressed out.

"Hey," I say. I touch my fingertip to her chin and angle her face toward mine. Our noses touch, and I kiss along the familiar band of freckles that runs along hers. "You. *You* are my family."

She nods, because it's all she can do. We've been down the family road more times than I can count in the last few months.

Because I want to be sure this feels like family for her. That *I* feel like family for her.

We've settled into our one-bedroom studio in Southern California, right down the hall from her brother, Carter. And Quinn...well, for once, she seems happy. Content. Safe. *Grounded.*

"I just..." Quinn says, accidentally squeezing the icing bag so hard, she leaves a blob of the stuff on the pie. Quinn lets out a gasp and starts to do damage control, and I watch her turn a gooey blob of cream into this gorgeous flower with quick precision. When it's all better, she sinks back against the edge of the counter, but her relief only lasts a second. She looks at me and holds her frosting smeared hands up in defeat. "I just…"

I press my index finger to her lips.

"Don't. Seriously. Just don't. Let's enjoy this. It's our first Thanksgiving here." I take in the apartment, small as it may be. Its walls are covered in my photos and shelves lined with Quinn's favorite cookbooks. We've made it our home, and I feel a sense of pride in that, because I feel like even though she lived in a nice place with her parents before this, that this is her first real *home*. The first place that she can just be her and it's okay. Better than okay, because we're together. At least for now.

Fuck, why do I keep thinking things like that? It's just a month. It's nothing in the grand scheme, right?

"Okay," she says. She checks her watch, the face fogged with smeared icing. "My brother and Shayna won't be here for another thirty minutes. I mean, if there was anything else you wanted to do…until then…"

I don't wait for anything else. I wrap my arm around her waist and pick her up until her back is against the wall and push my lips onto hers. "Like what?"

She playfully jerks her head toward our bedroom. I shake my head.

"Nope.You.Here.*Now*," I growl.

I hoist her up, and she wraps her legs around my waist just as I slam her back into the wall. *Gently*, of course. No more begging her to stop before she pushes me too far. In this new life, she's all mine.

I pull her hair back away from her face and kiss her throat. "You're beautiful," I say.

"I love you," she says. And as the words tumble from her lips, they squeeze at my heart just like they do every single time she utters them, because I know exactly how lucky I am—*we are*—to be right here. "But you're going to have to be quick."

"Quick I can do," I say, lifting her hand and licking frosting off her fingers.

"Don't I know it." Quinn winks.

"Just for that, you're getting a long session…in the bedroom."

I carry her into our bedroom and let her fall back onto the mattress, and start working on the buttons on her shirt.

"We don't have time for all that," Quinn says, swatting my hand away. She reaches out and undoes my belt. She doesn't quite get it all the way undone before my phone starts buzzing in my pocket.

"Don't even think about it," she says, her glare so sexy, I'm glad the phone buzzed when it did.

"Never." I grin.

She reaches into my jeans for the phone. Maybe she plans to toss it across the room. Or onto the nightstand. Or even out the window. Right now, I don't really care where the hell it ends up. I just want her, as soon as humanly possible.

But instead, Quinn stops.

She holds the phone out a little and her brow pulls down, like she's focusing hard, making sure her eyes are seeing it right.

"Baby? What is it?" I ask. I reach out for the phone, but she yanks it back. She crawls backward off of the bed and stands several feet away from me.

"Why is *Caroline* calling you? Today?"

Two

QUINN

Ben frowns back at me. His eyebrows are pulled together in confusion, or annoyance, or maybe a thin line between the two. "I have no idea, Quinn. Come back over here."

But I don't. Instead, I clutch the phone closer to my chest and shake my head. I don't understand why things can't just be okay. Why in the middle of our first holiday in this apartment is his ex-girlfriend calling? The same ex-girlfriend whose appearance spiraled our relationship out of control last year?

"Quinn, if you want to know why she's calling, just answer the phone. I don't know, and I sure as shit don't have anything to talk to her about."

I roll the phone back and forth in my hands and consider his words. I take two steps toward him. His dark eyes and the small nod he gives tell me he gets that it's hard for me to take steps forward, rather than running.

"Or, just ignore it, and come back over here. I promise I can make you forget." He reaches out and links his index finger through my belt loop and pulls me back into him. I don't push away. We spent so much of our past with me yanking back and Ben grasping for me.

"I'm sure it's just because it's a holiday...right?" I hate the jittery shake in my voice.

"Mmhmm," He murmurs against my mouth.

"But like, has she called before?"

"Quinn." Ben rolls his head around and sighs like he wishes to god I'd let this go. "She may have called once or twice. But I never answer. I think she's just lonely."

"And?" I press him back, hold out for more. I want to know why the hell this is all coming up and out now and if any of it ever would have if I never saw that call. And then I wonder if any of it matters.

And I realize that, even if it doesn't matter to Ben, it matters to me. It matters whether I want it to or not. And I hate that.

But at least I'm not running away from it.

Though running would feel so...clear. So freeing. This is messy as hell.

"And Caroline doesn't have a ton of friends." I hate that I can relate to her at all, but in that way, I can. "But you," he says. He pulls me in and his thumbs rub circles on my hip bones making me shiver. "You've just got to trust me."

"I—"

The knock at the door interrupts us.

"That's my brother," I say, half truly reluctant to answer the door, and half completely relieved to have an excuse to end this for now. Ben just stares up at me like he's contemplating pretending we aren't home like we've done before. "We should, like, go answer that…"

Ben laughs and stands up to adjust himself while I re-button my flannel shirt. "Hey.' He stops me in the doorway of our bedroom.

"I love you, Quinn."

And I believe him. I do.

"Shayna, what is that?" I ask, trying to swallow a laugh. My brothers' girlfriend rolls her eyes and sets the pan full of burnt crust onto the counter top.

"Peach pie, obvs," she says, gesturing to the murky goo with a confused smile. "I thought it'd make it feel more like home." Her voice drops off a little. I want to say something snarky, but Shayna looks sincere. She's really the only one of us in the room that has a family worth going home to for the holiday, and, instead, she chose to spend it with us assholes.

Shayna showed up in Southern California a few months ago wanting to spend her summer here rather than in the soaking humidity of Georgia and has pretty much been a permanent fixture ever since. Plus, she sort of helped Carter get sober, so I owe her. She and Carter have a complicated relationship, in that she is completely into him and he isn't ready to settle down with anyone, especially since he just stopped drinking, but Shayna makes him happy so she stays.

"Ben, you want to watch the game?" Carter asks, looking at the kitchen he so doesn't want to be stuck in with a weird panic.

Ben scoffs. "Really, dude?" He jokes because sports are so not his thing, but he follows Carter into the living room anyway as a mercy gesture.

"So, what's up with you two?" Shayna leans over the countertop and watches me scoop the stuffing out of the way-too-big turkey, settling in for the conspiratorial chat Carter knew was coming and was desperate to avoid at any cost.

"What do you mean?" I am taking an unfair amount of aggression out on the innocent turkey hanging on my counter.

She applies a slow coat of lip gloss and scoots a little closer, pushing a bowl of cranberries out of the way with her newly manicured finger. "I mean, he's usually attached to your hip. But he's in there watching golf or something."

"Football," I correct with a snicker.

"Whatever. What's going on?" She raises an eyebrow and bumps her hip against mine, like in solidarity. That one tiny gesture gets me to put down the stuffing and consider letting it all spill. Without my high school best friend, Sydney, around and with no real friends other than Ben here, I've been lonely. Shayna's olive branch is so damn tempting right now, it's sad.

I inhale sharply. I could tell Shayna that Caroline called. I could. She'd understand. She'd probably even call her back. But Ben told me to trust him, and I do. *I have to.* Because doing anything else only proves that I haven't changed, and I think I have. I hope I have. I don't want to ruin this bubble of perfection by being the girl I used to be.

"Do you eat sweet potatoes?" I ask Shayna.

"Huh?" At the question she purses her shiny lips and narrows her eyes.

"Sweet potatoes? Do you like them? I made a sweet-potato soufflé. I've never made it before, but if, you know, if they're not your favorite then who gives a crap if I screwed it up, right? Ben says he can take them or leave them—"

"Quinn, cut the crap. What's going on?" She leans forward, her long hair grazing the counter with the food on it. She doesn't seem to notice. Or care.

I stab at the bowl of stuffing with my fork. "Ben's ex."

Shayna smiles and drags her eyebrows together all at the same time. "What about her? Wait, you're not worried about her are you?"

"She called today," I admit, my voice revealing every petty, stupid thing I've been trying to pretend I don't feel since the call came through.

"What'd she want?" Shayna asks, her eyes sharp on me.

"I don't know. He didn't answer. But why is she calling at all?" I shove the stuffing bowl away and brace my hands on the counter.

Shayna looks over her shoulder toward where the guys are sitting on the couch, Ben silent and confused, Carter jumping up and screaming at the TV every minute or two. "Has she before?"

"He says he isn't sure. Maybe." I follow Shayna's line of sight and try not to focus on how much I love Ben's confused face. I need to clear my head, and getting dopey over how he frowns just a tiny bit when he's watching a football game isn't helping.

"Do you believe him?" The question is wide open, and I know Shayna won't judge me no matter how I answer.

"Why would he lie? She's all the way in Kentucky. He's here with me. There's nothing to worry about, right?" I whirl back to the oven and start the laborious process of jamming remaining dishes that need to be warmed into the tiny appliance, glad for the sweaty, frustrating distraction.

Shayna comes to the side of the oven to watch me and shrugs. "I don't know. Sometimes, people don't need a reason to lie. They just can't help themselves." Have I mentioned that Shayna is a psych major? She throws out these helpful, paranoia-inducing tidbits all of the time.

"Ben isn't like that," I say as I manage to wrestle the oven door shut with a satisfying slam, smoothing the wrinkles in my apron, trying to iron out my nerves in the process.

"Let's hope not." Shayna pipes leftover icing onto the tip of her finger in neat little swirls and eats it off.

So much for a friend to take the place of Syd. What I wouldn't give for my sweet bestie's nauseatingly sunny spin on life right now. This is payback for all the times I gleefully rained on her little optimism parades just to be a sour asshat. "Thanks for the confidence-building talk, Shayna. I can tell you'll go far in your chosen profession."

"The truth hurts, baby," Shayna says with a wink as she consumes dangerous amounts of icing. I don't smile back. She tosses the icing bag aside and tilts her head down to see my face.

"Oh, come on, you know I'm kidding. For whatever reason, Ben is crazy about you. You guys have a good thing going here. Don't blow it with your insecurity, Quinn."

"I'm not insecure." *Maybe if I say it enough times, it'll be true.*

"Right." Shayna rolls her eyes dramatically. "Because women that are completely secure in their relationships worry about girls that are a thousand miles away." Shayna continues her random pre-dinner grazing session by biting into a carrot stick, and I will her to choke on it.

"Caroline just has this whole 'babe-in-the-woods' act down. And I'm not buying it. I'm just not sure Ben sees that."

"Quinn. Get a grip. Seriously. You're leaving soon, don't ruin the last few days you have with Ben before Italy stressing over a non-issue. Freak." Shayna mutters the last word under her breath. Shayna is the closest friend I have, but her version of 'keeping-it-real' seriously makes me hate her sometimes. I miss Sydney so much it aches. She would empathize with me over all these inane problems and always tell me what I wanted to hear—which I love about her—and miss so much right now. But I'm glad Syd is where she is, even if it isn't near me—she's coaching gymnastics in Texas, engaged to Grant. Safe and happy, just like she always deserved. I know I always made fun of her upbeat belief in happily ever after, but I'm so glad she got hers, it makes my heart squeeze.

God, I miss her.

"It's time to eat," I say, stabbing a knife into the peach pie. "Oh, and Shayna, I hope you get all of the hair in your food."

Three

BEN

Quinn kicks me like a mule for the twelfth time in her sleep before I get up out of bed. As soon as I'm up, she stretches out like it's what she's been waiting for—to have the entire space to herself.

It used to be that she couldn't sleep without me next to her. She would form herself to my side and fall asleep on my chest every single night, clutching onto my t-shirt. But I guess most fears wither that way, and I have gone from being something Quinn isn't sure will be there in the morning to something she counts on to be there without fail. Quinn used to cling to me for dear life. But slowly, her grip has loosened. Slowly she's begun to trust that I'm not going to go anywhere.

I rummage around my nightstand for my keys and grab my camera as I slip on flip flops. In November. And stumble out the door, locking it behind me.

I get in the car and drive, rolling the windows down in the chill of the early morning because I love the way the cold air opens my lungs and clears my mind. I love the way it smells here so much, it's weird to think I didn't even know this smell existed a few months ago.

This whole move has been exciting and weird and huge. When we first moved here, it felt like total culture shock. We didn't exactly live in the sticks before, but the change in pace was the biggest difference. We went from our slow-as-hell town where the only things going on were midnight showings of old movies, or driving into the city. But in California, there's always something going on, and for the first couple of months, we were blowing and going like the two irresponsible kids our parents always told us that we were. Going to festivals across the state—even if they were devoted to avocados-- or food trucks that specialized in fish tacos, or to watch professional sand castle competitions, or listen to free shows by wild bands in all kinds of parks…we wanted to see it all—together. We've settled down, not only because we quickly learned just how far our extra financial aid money *wouldn't* stretch, but because once we got our tiny apartment set up, there was nowhere else in the world we'd rather be.

I pull down the highway, knowing exactly where I want to be. I only have a limited amount of time, but I try not to speed, not to make any stupid mistakes that will put us in jeopardy. The last thing we need right now is a ticket or a fender-bender. Not that we're doing so badly; but if we want to get ahead, we need to keep on our toes. Quinn's been in culinary school and working part time at an Italian joint. I'm finishing up my degree in Digital Photography, and working as a photographer's assistant. It sounds glamorous, but in reality, I'm really just a baby wrangler. I make a kids laugh, run or play so that their parent can have the perfect photo to mount above their fireplace. But what I really love to take photos of are the quieter moments--ones that don't contain mini sweater vests, infant bow ties and orchestrated smiles.

When I get to the spot where I need to be, I park the car, get out my gear, and set up my tripod, put my camera in manual mode and adjust the intervalometer to take a photograph every second. I probably look like a huge creeper up here on a dark overpass, but I've wanted to get a good time lapsed sequence of traffic on the freeway since we got to California. The constant ticking of the camera is the most calming sound in the world.

Normally. Right now, I can't stop wondering why Caroline has been calling lately. I pull out my phone and rub my thumb on the glass of the screen.

What's the harm in calling her back and seeing if everything is okay? Just to see if she needed something? I scroll through the call log until I get to her number.

What's wrong is that it's not my problem whether everything is okay with Caroline or not. If I call her back, Quinn will lose her shit. And *that is* my problem.

Quinn's leaving soon, and I can't ditch the feeling that there's something more behind her going. How could she not even know the trip was a possibility, and why did she wait so damn long to tell me about it? Whatever is going on, it's not going to get any better with me leaving in the middle of the night like this anymore.

I stuff my phone back into my pocket and decide to go home. To Quinn. Where I belong.

When I get back to our apartment, I kick off my shoes and one goes astray and hits the baseboard. Quinn rolls over and rubs her eyes.

"Hey," she says. Her voice is thick with sleep and incredibly sexy.

"Sorry." I lean across the bed and kiss her on the forehead. "I didn't mean to wake you."

"What time is it?" She rubs her hand along my bicep without opening her eyes.

"About four," I say, watching her hand on my arm in the shadowy dark.

Quinn groans and nestles closer. "You're cold. Wait, were you out?"

"Couldn't sleep." I run my free hand over her shoulder, letting the backs of my fingers trail up and down her arm.

"So, where'd you go?" Her voice is getting clearer, like she was talking underwater and is now breaking through the surface.

"Went to shoot some," I say, holding up my camera as evidence.

"Right," she says. Her mouth forms a tight line, and this is all the worst kind of déjà vu.

"What?" I ask. She sits up, pulls the blanket up to her chest, and shakes her head, avoiding me, avoiding this conversation. "You were sleeping like crap, something wrong?"

Quinn gives a quick nod that isn't even half an answer.

"Are you still upset about Caroline calling? Because I told you it's nothing." I cup her elbow in my palm, amazed by how small and delicate it is. Realizing little details like this about her just before she's about to leave chokes me with a regret I can't shake. It's almost like I'm scared I might lose her, might lose the chance to discover all the little amazing things about her I haven't had the time to find out about yet.

"I believe you. I do. It's weird that like, after all this time, she still has this connection to you, but, I don't know, I trust you." She sits up, the covers draped over her shoulders like a cloak.

I pull her to me and kiss her on the lips, hard and thankful. "Good." And now I'm damn glad I didn't call her back.

"Are you hungry?" she asks.

I shake my head as I stash my camera back in its case. "You sure something else isn't up? You seem like there's something more you want to say" She fidgets some more, stares at her hands, lets out a big breath, and then clamps her mouth shut again. If I didn't love her so much, this routine would be infuriating. "Just say it, Quinn."

"Are you sure? It doesn't have to be leftovers from dinner. I can make you whatever you want. Frittata? French toast?" Her voice gets high and flighty as she rattles off food suggestions.

"Jesus, Quinn, you sound like my mom." I shake off the annoyance I feel building, push out a deep breath and start again. "No, I don't want anything to eat. I want you to freaking talk to me."

She jerks her head back at the mention of my mom. I seldom talk about my parents, or even say their names.

"It's just…I have this…Never mind. It's stupid." Quinn pulls her arms up inside the sleeves of her sweatshirt and purses her lips.

"Would you relax?" I sit down next to her on the bed and trace her collar bone with my index finger. "Quinn, baby, I've seen you naked. You can talk to me."

She continues to coil into herself, and I know it's because, for Quinn, clothes off is easier than walls down.

"Quinn." I slide my hands on either side of her face so that she's looking at me.

She pulls back gently and presses the heels of her hands over her eyebrows for a long few seconds. "I just have this fear that things are changing. You're gone a lot taking pictures, and I love that you do that, and I'm about to leave for Italy, and... Okay, so this thing with Caroline—"

"There is no *thing* with Caroline, Quinn." I say it, but I don't really know if it's true or not. I don't know why she's calling, I don't know if something is wrong and I'd be lying if I said it wasn't eating at me.

"But there is. Because she's calling, and it freaks me out." Her voice and her hands and her eyelashes all kind of flutter, like she's about to crack into a million pieces.

No.

I'm here.

With Quinn.

Caroline and whatever is up with her doesn't matter.

I pull her into my arms and the fluttering stops. I love the solid, steady feel of her against me.

"Why would that worry you? I'm here. With you. Always."

Four
QUINN

I wad my apron into a ball, cram it into my locker and slam the metal door shut. "I'll see you soon," I say to my boss, Teresa.

"It's going to be amazing," she says. You can practically see the glossy cannoli cream shining in her eyes. "And don't you worry about your job; it's here waiting for you. Just don't forget about us all while you're gone."

I want to roll my eyes, because this job is nothing worth remembering, but I know how damn lucky I am to have this chance to see the world and learn something new— and not be stuck in my forties and working in this knock-off brand Italian food chain—like Teresa, who would give anything for the chance I have thrown at my feet.

"I won't," I say. I pull my hoodie over my head and grab my purse off of the bench. "I have to get going. Ben says he has something planned for tonight."

"Of course, have fun."

Teresa hired me the first week I arrived in California. Ben and I had no plan other than that we were saying to hell with our parents' theory that art school is for delinquents, and we were going to make it work out here on our own—with the help of massive student loans that'd we would probably be paying off until we were near death.

"Holy mother of tinsel, what's going on?" I ask. I stop in the doorway of our apartment to take it all in. There's a small artificial Christmas tree in the corner, decorated with big bows that look like they're threatening to topple the whole damn thing. There's a poinsettia on our cluttered coffee table, garland above the doorway to our bedroom, and the whole place reeks of those cinnamon-infused pinecones.

I turn to Ben, who is smirking like he has a secret. "What's all this?"

"Christmas," he says with a quick shrug on his shoulders. His voice is a little shy, like he isn't sure if I'll approve. His coy expression is adorable, and I can't help think of the Christmas we spent in Georgia together the night we got back together after the whole Mark fiasco. The night he had me practically begging him to kiss me. He did. And more.

That night marked the first time I felt something other than the need to be self-destructive. Ben has brought more to my life than just being a boyfriend. He's brought stability, and a beautiful love that I never imagined I could deserve.

I smile back at him, because I know he's remembering that night, too.

He winks at me and I feel the familiar butterflies in my stomach take flight. I clear my throat. "Wow, you really went all out, guys," I say, finally admitting that my brother and Shayna are also in this perfect Christmas romance bubble.

"It was all Shayna," Ben says.

"Obviously she knew it was me. I bet you two half-wits wouldn't know a Douglas Fir from a Noble."

"And you'd be right about that," Carter says with a laugh. He reaches over, hooks his arm around Shayna's waist and pulls her into his side and kisses her ear. I've never seen my brother like this. I mean, I've seen him with girlfriends before, sure. But this brand of happiness and ease is new, especially since he started working full time at a small accounting firm and stopped drinking. It takes a lot for him to relax lately. I can't believe it took my former nemesis to bring out this side of him.

"Anyway," Shayna says, cozying closer to Carter while she gets her brag on. "I got a fake tree, because I didn't know if anyone would be here for Christmas, or if it would just sit here and die. So...Ben?" Shayna raises her eyebrows curiously and taps her foot.

"Huh?" Ben asks. I love that he was ignoring her because he was busy looking me over like he wanted everyone else in the room to disappear.

"Will you? Be here for Christmas?" Her question is so insistent, it borders on severely irritating despite her good elf act.

The guilt over missing Christmas with Ben churns in my

stomach. I can't believe he'll be sitting here alone. With that hideous tree Shayna decorated.

"I don't know what I'm doing yet, Shayna. But I promise you'll be the first to know."

Shayna squints her eyes at Ben's sarcasm.

"Anyway, there's hot cocoa and I picked up appetizers from that place on 5th, and I guess we'll eat now if you assholes are hungry, but if it were up to me—"

We all snicker and Carter grabs a wrapped box off of the table.

"Prezzies!" Shayna squeals. She rushes to Carter clapping like a damn seal. But way more annoying.

"I shouldn't even give this to you now. I'm going to see you on Christmas." Carter kisses her forehead and hands Shayna her gift.

"But we had to celebrate with Quinn and Ben." She grins and rips into the wrapping paper.

I feel Ben's arms wrap around my waist and slouch into him.

"I wish you would have told me you guys were planning this. I haven't had time to get gifts together." I frown.

"I've got a few ideas of things you could give me," Ben says, nipping at my ear with his teeth.

"Easy. We've got company," I laugh.

"We're not company," Carter says. "But dude, come on, that's my sister."

I don't blush often, but I can't fight the warmth rising up my neck and onto my face.

"You can bring us something back from Italy, Quinnlette," Shayna says, borrowing the nickname my brother coined for me when we were kids. "Preferably something sparkly."

"Right," I say. "I'm sure that will happen, Shay."

"Hey, is this not sparkly enough for you?" Carter asks, holding up Shayna's dainty wrist to display a stunning gold bracelet.

"It's gorgeous, babe. Merry Christmas to me!" Shayna stands on her tip-toes and kisses my brother. They're really riding the line of no longer being cute tonight, and leaning dangerously toward just being vomitously sickening.

"Hey, that's my brother," I joke.

"I think we want to go home and, um, open presents," Carter says, pulling Shayna to the door.

"Your gift is under the tree, Quinn. It's new pots and pans from all three of us. Not very original, but we had to do something to make sure you'd keep on cooking for us!" Shayna squeals in the high-pitched voice I seldom hear since we left high school on her way out the door.

"Well, that was a quick celebration," I say. I turn to Ben who has his right hand behind his back, like he's holding something. "What are you hiding back there?"

"Nothing," Ben smirks.

I take the last few steps toward him. "You don't have another gift for me, do you? Shayna said that one was from everyone. Ben?"

He pulls his hand out from behind his back. The click startles me and sudden flash blinds me momentarily.

"How many times have I told you I hate when you take my picture?"

He tosses his camera onto the sofa and pulls me in, his lips on my throat before I can argue any further.

"I know. I'm sorry," he says.

"No you're not." I find his lips with mine.

"You're right. I'm not. You're so damn beautiful, Quinn. And I'm going to miss you so damn much. I just want to remember this. Right now."

I can't argue with him.

"And this," he says, his lips working their way down my neck, shoulders, and chest. He drops to his knees and I have a momentary flash of panic.

Don't propose. Please. Don't. Propose.

"And this," he says, he lifts up the hem of the light cotton skirt that skims just above my knees, presses his mouth to my thigh and I can't help the moan that escapes my lips. His warm kisses and capable hands make their way up to the most sensitive skin until my knees are wobbling and my moans and gasps have turned into begging.

"We should go to bed," I whimper against Ben's lips

while tugging at his belt.

"You should let me take you right here," he says. He helps me with the unfastening of that stupid belt and shimmies out of his jeans.

"I think that's a better idea," I agree.

I pull his white t-shirt over his head, exposing his warm skin and run my hands over his chest, his abs, anything I can touch while he helps get rid of my pesky skirt and panties.

"I love you," I say as he grips my hips and slides inside of me.

"Love you, baby."

Ben and I here, making love next to a Christmas tree (albeit artificial) like we did that first time—that night I showed up at his house in that damn dress in the rain, makes me nostalgic for those early days before bills and jobs and real life. But it also makes me so content with where we are.

"Merry un-Christmas to me," I say, catching my breath. "That was way better than a bracelet, by the way."

"So, I do have something else for you," he says, brushing my bangs out of my face.

I feel myself deflate again. "Come on, it's bad enough I'm leaving you here alone for Christmas. Please, let's not do the whole, 'shower me with gifts,' thing."

"You need to go, Quinn. It's *Italy*. It's really okay. It'll be quiet here, yeah, but I'll study, and work, and stay up all night taking pictures without you getting mad at me." He grins, and if it reached up a fraction of a centimeter closer to his eyes, I'd almost believe it was a genuine smile.

"What about, maybe, going home with Shayna and Carter?" I say it slowly. Cautiously.

"To Georgia?" He loosens his grip on me ever so slightly, like he's trying to gauge whether or not I'm being serious.

I settle in his arms so that we're still locked together, but I can see his eyes, can look him full in the face and be the responsible, loving girlfriend he deserves. Or at least the most decent version of that particular girl I know how to be. "Yeah, I mean, I know we've all mentioned it, but really, Ben, I'm sure you're welcome to stay at my house with Carter—"

"I doubt that." His mouth twists in a wry grin, I'm sure over the thought of my parents' chilly, anti-social reaction to finding him on their doorstep, ruining their annual Christmas Eve blitz. *Ho ho ho.*

"Yeah, you're right. My parents are dicks, but yours…they love you, Ben." I push back all the rebellious anti-parent craziness we've been rallying since we left home, because I know how much he needs this. And I owe him. I know this entire thing severing from his parent's thing has been his way of staying by my side, and now it's time I paid him back by putting on my big girl pants.

"Quinn—"

"Look, I know things got crazy there with your mom. And

I can't even tell you how thankful I am that you didn't let her ultimatums stop you from being with me, because, this?" I gesture to us, lying naked on our living room floor, limbs intertwined. "This is pretty great."

"Agreed," Ben laughs and kisses the tip of my nose. "Doesn't get a whole hell of a lot better."

"But, I know she's got to miss you, Ben. Just think about it, okay?" I let out a breath, and I know he'll probably do more than think. There's a tiny fear that doing this, letting him go, is just giving him permission to fly away from me and back to the comforting arms of the people who love him and hate me and might, maybe, be able to show him just what a catastrophe his decision was.

Like they'd need much proof. The girl he ran away from everything for is leaving him high and dry on Christmas, for god's sake. His mother won't even have to lace this one in 'bless her hearts' this time. I suck and that's going to be clear, even to my biggest fan.

Even to Ben.

Which is why I have to show him that I do actually care.

"For you, baby, anything."

"So, what do you have for me?" I ask, peering around his long frame. Ben hoists himself off of the floor and disappears into our bedroom. "It's not more pictures of me, is it?" I call after him.

He returns moments later in boxers, holding a manila

envelope. "Hey, no fair on the clothes," I gripe.

"Fine," he grins and tosses me the t-shirt I'd torn off of him earlier. He waits for me to pull it over my head, then hands me the envelope.

"What's this?" I start to unclasp the brads holding the envelope shut, but Ben covers my hand with his.

"Wait, let me just explain this to you," he says. His voice quivers a little, and I don't really understand his nerves.

"My life is full of photographs. I mean, yeah..." Ben motions around to the walls covered with his black-and-white masterpieces. He swallows hard. "But there's the other kind, too. The snapshots in my mind that make everything else fade except that one moment. Some of them change everything for you. You and I, that first date I ever took you on in Savannah was one of those for me." He nudges my hands and I finish opening the envelope and pull out the single photo.

"Is this..?" I don't have to finish, I know exactly what the picture is. The ancient oak tree bends and dips toward the ground, its branches twisting and growing in each direction with thick Southern moss draped from every bit of it. It's the tree that we sat under sharing both delicious and scary food. The tree that Ben kissed me for the first time under. "It's beautiful."

"You're beautiful."

"Thank you," I say. "But wait, when did you take this?"

"When Carter and I went back to Georgia to get Shayna's stuff a few months ago."

"Ben, Savannah isn't exactly on the way to Atlanta. Like, at all."

Ben shrugs his shoulders. "I had him take a little detour. He understood it was for a good cause." I suddenly love my brother so much more than I did thirty minutes ago.

"I love it."

"I love you. And our lives. And this," he says, pointing to the tree in the photo, "this is what started it all. You changed everything for me in that moment."

The tears blur my vision, and my throat burns from me trying to keep them from falling.

"So much better than a bracelet," I say.

Five
QUINN

"Don't forget this," Ben says. "You'll definitely need it." He grins and tosses the paperback English-to-Italian translation book to me. I shove it into my carry-on, because I know not a single thing, no matter how small, will fit into my overflowing suitcase. I zip the bag closed and stare into the empty trunk of Ben's car. "Hey, you nervous?"

"More than a little," I admit.

"Don't be," he says. He pulls me in and wrapped up in his familiar, warm arms, leaving really seems like a completely terrible idea. "You're going to do great, and you'll be home before you even miss us."

"Are you going to be okay?" I ask, nestling against the solid wall of his chest. He does such an amazing job of always being okay, always being amazing, that I never really know if he truly is.

And I tend to do such a thorough job of being so not okay, we're usually focused on me. Or we were. That was the old Quinn and Ben. It's all different now.

"Quinn, I'll be fine. Let's get you inside, though. Otherwise you're going to miss this flight, and then you can thank Shayna and her dramatic good-bye this morning." It's true. Ben and I would have been here an hour ago if it weren't for Shayna showing up this morning with bagels and insisting that we have an AM version of the Last Supper together. Damn Carter for having a real job and getting to skip out on it.

"Let me take that," Ben says. He pulls the cross-body carry-on I have off of my shoulder and slings it over his, even though he's already lugging my suitcase for me.

"You don't have to do that, I can get it."

Ben stops walking, and shakes his head. "I know I don't *have* to, Quinn. I want to." It's not the words he says, it's in the way he says them— and the way he looks at the ground, rather than at me that makes me pause. Something isn't right. And it might be bigger than just my leaving.

A small pool of panic gurgles up in me, and soon it's welling so fast I feel like I'm going to drown in it.

I can't worry about this right now. I can't. If I do, I won't ever get on that plane. Maybe he's just nervous about me going. That's got to be it.

"Okay."

We continue to walk to my gate, Ben taking slower steps than me so that I can keep up with his long legs. It's quiet between us now. How many times can you say you'll miss each other, or 'I love you' before it just sounds redundant and loses a little sincerity? And the quiet is okay, because every once in a while, Ben extends his fingertips and brushes mine, and the familiarity of that calloused touch is all I need right now.

I wish, for once, the line at the ticket counter was longer. That they didn't print my boarding passes like it was a race, and toss my luggage onto that conveyer belt like it's perishable. Because before I have a chance to breathe, Ben is standing with me at the line for security. The line he can't cross.

"I wish you could walk me the entire way," I say. I can't swallow the stinging lump in my throat this time and tears spill over.

"Shhh. Baby, don't cry," Ben says. He wipes my cheeks with his thumbs. "We'll talk all the time. And you're going to be so busy and learning so much—"

"I know. That's the point. I'm doing all of this and you'll be sitting at home alone."

What started off as silent tears falling has turned into full-on idiotic sobbing.

Ben interrupts my theatrics with his signature raspy chuckle. "I can handle a little alone time, Quinn." He's smirking in a delicious way that I can't help but smile back at. I swipe at the stupid tears, trying my best to make them stop.

"What are you thinking?" I ask. I glance at the growing line at security, and then back to Ben and those gorgeous brown eyes that I don't want to leave yet. *Ever.*

"Quinn, there's a whole hell of a lot running through my mind right now, and absolutely none of it is G-rated, so you'd better get on that plane," Ben says. He grins and nods toward the line. He's trying to make it easier for me, but it doesn't help. I don't want to go. "Come here." He pulls me in and wraps his hand around the back of my neck, his fingers tangling into the low braid and kisses me.

"I love you," I say against his lips.

"I love you." It's the millionth time I've heard it, but it hasn't lost a single ounce of meaning for me. If anything, it feels like this time, this way, is a whole new version, and one I needed to hear at this exact moment. "Now go." His voice goes from achingly sweet to rough in an instant, like he's shooing some wild animal he tried to make his pet back home to the woods.

Ugh. Bad metaphor on so many levels.

I don't prolong the torture, just whirl around and rush away, not looking back, and knowing that he'll know it's not because I'm so excited or blasé or composed. It's because this is wrecking me. Finally, walking away from what I love is the hard thing for me, and it's immeasurably harder than I was prepared for. Walking away used to be this mix of sadness with a heavy dollop of relief. Now I feel weighted and gutted and torn apart all at once.

I make my way onto the plane and stare out the window at the tarmac, my hands gripped in my lap, and wait for stomach-dropping minute of time when my body is adjusting to leaving earth and hurtling through air. I wait for that minute so I can remember that the fear of something new is normal, but the stress of the last few days must be more than I anticipated, because I'm asleep before we even leave the ground.

The pilot's voice interrupts my catnap and I jerk upright in my seat and wipe the drool from the corner of my mouth. "I'd like to thank you all for traveling with us today, and would like to welcome you to Rome. I hope you'll enjoy your stay here, or wherever your final destination is."

The plane bumps along the runway, and the other passengers give the pilot a boisterous round of applause. I've never understood this concept. *Bravo on doing your job and not killing us, Captain!* Still, I feel my cynical heart melt a little bit at the announcement that we are officially on Italian soil.

Part of me feels like this can't even be real. Because people like me don't get these types of opportunities. Screw ups don't end up with guys like Ben. Or in Italy.

Except it has actually happened. Ben is mine, and I'm *here.*

It isn't long before I've collected my luggage, boarded the sleek yellow and white EuroStar train, and have arrived in my home for the next month- Spello.

I collect my large, red suitcase and head out of the train station in search of the home I'll be staying in. There are only a handful of students in the program, so we're each staying with a resident of the tiny as hell town. I stop on the steps outside of the station and take in the gorgeous little hilltop medieval town.

The sun is high and bright, and the sky is a pure, sweet blue. The entire town seems baked by the sun's glow, and there's this kind of bleached-clean beauty that makes even the occasional broken shutter and toppled garbage can with its rolling green wine bottle seem quaint. Its cute laned ways are filled with potted flowers, so spots of red and pink and white add pretty bursts to the cracking stone steps. The cobbled streets are as treacherous as they are gorgeous, with missing stones and uneven, jutting shards and deep cracks. The ancient brick and stone houses don't feel like they should have satellite dishes and plastic watering cans and mail boxes full of bills, but they do, of course. As much as they seem like bizarre relics of ancient history to me, for everyone who lives in them, they're just home.

There are endless vistas of rolling hills dotted with brown and green trees and stone archways carved with intricate designs and Latin inscriptions. I've never seen anything like it in my life, and I feel like I could have traveled in a tornado or through a wardrobe to get here. How the hell is this only a plane ride away from my normal life?

I pull my map out of my purse, though I seriously doubt I'll need it in a town this small, and start up the cobbled walkway, careful not to break my ass. The lane curves and twists up the hillside, and I am so thankful for my laidback attire by the time I reach the stone villa. I knock lightly once, then again, but there isn't an answer at the door.

Crap.

I dig through my carry-on bag and pull out the wadded up piece of paper with the address and double check that I'm at the right place. I don't know how to get to the back of the house, and I don't want to stand out front. That only leaves one option.

Find food.

The bell above the door jingles as I push through it. I barely take a single step inside the small shop before I'm greeted by the most amazing medley of smells my nose has ever met— garlic and herbs and meat and bread. Sweet and savory scents intertwine in ways that shouldn't meld together and smell like heaven— but do. The stone walls are lined from floor-to-ceiling with dark wood shelves stocked full of wine bottles, so high that there's a ladder propped against the shelves to reach the top items. There's a crystal chandelier hanging in the center of the room that should overpower the small space, but it doesn't. Everything about the space is contradictory, yet perfect.

"*Buonasera!*" I female voice calls from behind the long counter.

"*Buongiorno!*" I reply. My Italian accent is severely lacking, but it's one of the three-or-so phrases I was able to learn before leaving. I walk to the side of the store that the voice came from, stopping to inhale deeply with every single step. The smells only intensify the empty, gnawing feeling in my stomach. I haven't had anything to eat since the bag of pretzels on my first plane ride this morning. When I pass the massive display of cheese wheels, I'm surprised by the woman who greets me. I expected someone older based on the voice when I came in.

Instead, a perfectly curvy, olive-skinned woman in her thirties, I would guess, is sitting behind the counter next to an industrial meat slicer.

"*Posso aiutarla?*" she says.

I wring my palms together like I'm dry washing them and bite my lip. "*Posso aiutarla?*" I repeat back, the words fumbling off of my tongue in my bastardized version of the language.

The woman puffs her cheeks and blows out a big breath in annoyance. "I said, may I help you?"

I let out a shaky laugh, "Oh, thank god you speak English."

She nods and wipes her hands on the front of her

apron. "I do."

"I'm sorry, I just…I didn't have a lot of notice before this trip, and I don't speak a lot of Italian. Or any. Or whatever."

"You are with the American school?" she asks.

I nod and take a few steps toward her. "I just got here, but my room isn't ready."

"You arrived early. I was going to go home to let you in when I left for *siesta*. Sit down, I'll make you a sandwich while you wait."

"Are you the owner of the Bianchi house?"

"*Si*."

"I'm Quinn," I say. I offer my hand to shake, but she leans in and kisses each of my cheeks instead. It should be weird. I hate having people up in my bubble, but it doesn't feel awkward. Instead, it feels friendly and comfortable.

"Amalea," she says. "Sit." She motions to the round, rod-iron table in the corner of the small shop and I do as I'm told. I stare up at the handwritten menu and find myself fighting the urge to run away right now, before I've even been to a single day of class. Because I can't read a single word of that menu, and how the hell am I supposed to make it here for two months? "Would you like a drink?" Amalea asks, interrupting my internal-panic-attack.

"Cappuccino, please," I answer.

She shakes her head and makes a *'tisk-tisk'* noise with

her tongue. "I'll make you a *Caffè alla Nocciola.*"

Shit, I already forgot the one rule Carter told me before I left: never order a cappuccino after eleven AM, or you'll look like an asshole tourist. I nod appreciatively even though I don't have the slightest clue what she just offered me. I do know that she just placed the most incredible looking sandwich I've ever laid eyes on onto the table, and it's all I can do to not grab the thing and start tearing into it like an animal.

"This looks incredible, thank you." I pick up the flaky Panini-style sandwich full of cured meat and creamy cheese and pesto oozing gorgeously out of the sides and I take a less than lady-like sized bite. "Oh my god, this *tastes* incredible."

"*Prego*," Amalea says. "You finish eating and I'll take you to the house."

Amalea wanders back behind the counter, and I devour my sandwich.

I slide my cell phone out of my pocket, and frown when I realize I have next-to-no signal. Figures. I seriously doubt there are any cell towers remotely close to Spello, which I guess is okay, because from the itinerary that the school gave me, it doesn't look like I'll have a whole lot of time for social stuff. Ben will understand. As much as we love being together, one thing I'll never have to explain to Ben is getting lost in my art. It's the same reason I let him off the hook night after night when he drags his cold ass to bed at ungodly hours and his chilly skin shocks me out of deep sleep. I get needing that release, having to answer that call. If I can forgive his freezing feet on my calves in the dead of night, he can forgive my craptastic cell service and need to devote myself to herb blends and the perfect homemade pasta consistency.

After Amalea closes up the shop, we make the short walk back to her home, passing a woman selling flowers, a man selling cheese, and a stray chicken, but little else.

"You live here alone?" I ask Amalea as she shows me up the tiny, narrow staircase to my room. It's the only room on the second floor and it's dark and poorly insulated. The weather outside is gorgeous, but inside the room it's several degrees cooler. I hug myself to keep warm, hoping my discomfort isn't obvious. There's a single, thin blanket draped over the foot of the bed, and I make a mental note to try to find a street vendor that sells down comforters.

"I do," she says.

I scanned the walls when I came in, looking for photos that might tell me more about the woman I'll be sharing space with for the next few weeks. It's a habit, thanks to Ben, to notice people's photos, to try to dissect their lives based on those images. But other than a few religious pieces, Amalea's walls were bare.

"Must be quiet," I say. Idiot. It's obviously quiet. Which reminds me, it's also quiet for Ben, who is stuck at home alone.

"Do you mind if I make a call?" I ask. "Actually, do you know where I can get a decent signal?" I hold up my iPhone. While I get that calls will be limited, all decent girlfriends call their boyfriends to let them know when they've arrived safely in a foreign country. Even I know that.

"Try the roof," Amalea says. She points out of the room into the cramped space outside my bedroom. There's a small cutout in the ceiling that I didn't notice on the way up the stairs. That explains the draft. "Pull that chair over if you need a boost."

I wait until Amalea has left me in the space, and then do as she suggested, and slide the flimsy desk chair over to the hole in the ceiling and hoist myself up through it.

The sun setting over the town looks like it is straight out of a movie as I crawl through the tiny space. I hold the phone up toward the sky, squinting to see the screen with the glare of the last bit of daylight. Sure enough, three solid bars. I don't bother trying to calculate the time change because I know Ben will be waiting to hear how my flight was.

But he doesn't pick up.

His voicemail message is one of the prerecorded deals, so I don't even get to hear his voice. Though, I'd never admit that I miss his voice already— it hasn't even been an entire day.

"Hi, it's me. So, I'm here. And it's beautiful. And I'm watching the sunset and remembering how I said I never wanted to miss another sunset with you. So, I guess since I'm leaving you a message, you're sort of here with me. Or not. That sounds really stupid. Okay. Well, I love you. I'll call again soon."

I hang up the phone with more of that itching inside of me that says things are changing. Only now, even though I'm here, in Italy, it doesn't feel like it's changing for the better. I stand on the rooftop for a moment longer and take in the incredible view of the medieval village and gorgeous orchards, and gulp in a few deep breaths of fresh, Italian air to try to push my panic away. Because Ben in solid. He loves me. And I have to believe we're okay.

Six

BEN

I don't have school because of the holidays, and Ron, the photographer I work for, is on vacation, so there isn't any work to do. I head into the studio anyway to develop a few rolls of film I've been carrying around for a while. I'm lucky to have found a boss who still has an actual darkroom and uses real film to take photographs, even if he shoots all digital for his clients.

I eat lunch while I wait for the film to process, then go set up in the darkroom. I pull out the trays and line them up on the long table in the center of the room, then measure out the developer, stop, and fixer. I secure the first strip of negatives in the negative carrier, slide it into the enlarger, and flip the light of the enlarger on. After adjusting the focus nobs, the first image comes into focus.

It's Quinn. Caught off-guard the day we celebrated Christmas. Her lips are curled up into a snarky smirk that makes her look both annoyed and gorgeous.

Seeing her reminds me of the last time I was in this room.

I don't have a chance to use the darkroom unless Ron is out of town. That weekend he was up in San Simeon for his sister's wedding. Quinn and I had just finished finals that week and hadn't seen a lot of each other, so she tagged along. She helped me mix the chemicals and wash the prints, but mostly just sat on the counter and talked to me while I worked. I asked her to refill one of the trays with fresh water for me while I worked on dodging the shadows in a photo of a couple of kids at the beach. I glanced over my shoulder and saw Quinn leaning over the stainless table and even in the dim, red light I could make out all of her sweet curves, or maybe I just had them memorized.

"Why don't you move that tray over to the left a little more, it'd be a better place for it," I said.

"This one?" Quinn asked, pointing to the stop bath.

"Sure." I smiled.

"Yes, or no, Ben? *Sure* isn't really a—" She shook her head and laughed. "Oh, I see what you're doing there."

Quinn walked toward me, that brow arched in the confident way that turned me on every single time. Once she was within arm's reach, I hooked my arm around her waist and pulled her in to me. Our lips easily captured each other's, even in the near darkness, as if by instinct they knew just where to go.

My hands wandered under the back of her shirt, unhooking her bra and then across the soft skin of her flat stomach and up to her breasts. I pushed her shirt up over her head and then caught one of her nipples between my fingers teasingly. Quinn arched her back and let out a soft moan that made my body explode with desire and raw lust. Her hands worked their way down to my jeans, unzipping them and pushing them to the floor as I alternated between sucking and tugging on those perfect, pink nipples.

"What are you doing?" I asked. Quinn's mouth was on my throat, but her hands were fumbling with something behind us.

"This," she said. The room was drained of any light that had been as Quinn flipped the dim, red light off. I ran my hands up and down the length of her tiny body, pushing the thin cotton shorts to the floor. I slid her panties out of the way and was finally able to feel just how ready she was.

Every touch was intensified being in the total darkness like this. I never knew where Quinn's hands would end up next and the anticipation of the next kiss or touch was incredible. She would suck on my neck one minute and then I'd feel her lips on my chest. I was quickly learning not to even attempt to guess where she'd be next. But I wanted her. I wanted her so fucking badly. She pulled away for the briefest of seconds and I felt myself ache for more of her and my body shook with want.

"Who told you to hold back?" she said.

So I didn't.

Fuck, I miss my girlfriend.

I miss her, but there's still this part of me that feels like I need to let her go at this alone. I'm not ignoring her calls on purpose...I just haven't called her back. *Yet.* I will. It's like hearing her so far away is harder than not hearing from her at all. It's easier to pretend that she's waiting for me at home or will be home from work soon than to hear the thousands of miles between us on the other end of the phone.

I decide to pack up my gear and head home, but as I'm locking up, my phone vibrates in my hand.

"Hello," I say.

"Ben, it's Ron, how's things?"

"Doing okay, just leaving the shop, I was up here using the darkroom. Is that okay?"

"Course," he says. "Listen, I'm sure you have somewhere to be, but quickly, I wanted to talk to you about the sunsets."

"The sunsets?" I toss my camera bag into my back seat and start up my car.

"When you applied for the job with me, you brought in a portfolio of sunsets," Ron says. The ones I took for Quinn while we were apart all of those months.

"Right," I say.

"I have a friend up North here, that is looking to acquire a sequence of photos of sunsets, he wants to have them made into a collage and sold as posters. I vouched for your work, told him it's exactly what he's looking for. What do you think?"

I put the car back into park, trying to replay what Ron has just said, trying to process it.

"So, he wants to buy my work?"

"Yep."

"All of them?"

"Yep," Ron confirms. "So, I told him I'd check with you and give him your contact info, he should be in touch soon, he'd like to get this all wrapped up in the next few weeks."

I swallow hard and get a handle on my voice, which I know is going to shake with excitement. This is exactly what I've been waiting for. One tiny part of me is disappointed that

Quinn isn't here, waiting with wide eyes and bitten lips for me to fill her in. She won't be here when I click off to kiss me and offer her congratulations, to celebrate the changes that are coming. For both of us.

But this is happy. This is awesome news. And I'm legitimately happy when I say the next words. And maybe it's a good thing that Quinn is in Italy and this moment has already lost some of its luster. I exchange uncontrollable excitement for the kind of calm professionalism that might help me line up more jobs in the future. Which is the ultimate goal anyway.

"That sounds perfect. Yes, tell him that I said yes."

Seven

QUINN

"Buonasera!" I call into the tiny house before opening the door the rest of the way.

"Buonasera!" Amalea's now familiar voice replies. I've been in Italy for just over two weeks now. I love it here and can't wait to come back someday with Ben. Maybe even bring Carter and Shayna along. But school is rough. The courses aren't hard, necessarily, as much as I feel out of place. For starters, I'm the only girl in the classes, which is fine. I tend to relate to guys much better, but these guys are different. There are three of them, and their senses of humor are severely lacking. One of them, John Paul, he's from the United States, too, he says *"ci, ci!"* no less than one hundred times per class, and I'm pretty convinced that that phrase doesn't mean what he thinks it means. None of it is bad, it's just not comfortable. I'm much more content in Amalea's kitchen, helping her bake or clean, or just watching her conjure up these delicious meals all from recipes passed down to her from her family, never a written recipe in sight.

The kitchen is exactly where I find her now, stretching a large piece of dough out onto her simple, wooden counter top. "You're finished for the day already?" she asks.

"Yep. I have an early class tomorrow, though. What are you making?"

"Sfogliatelle." She lifts the buttery dough up, stretching it from underneath until it's paper thin and so beautiful. *Like magic.* "Have you eaten?"

"I nod. We made gnocchi with wild boar sauce."

"Ah, Chef Baldassare's favorite." Amelia doesn't look up from the dough she is tediously working when she says it. Maybe it's my imagination, but I think she works it a little harder.

"You know Chef? Of course you do, there's like, twenty people total in this town."

Amalea bites her bottom lip.

"I like him, which is saying something, because I don't like most people."

Amalea glances up, her brows pulled together. I'm either confusing or offending her. I rush to erase my social blunder as best I can, but I'm like a little kid scrubbing so hard on a mistake that I just wind up tearing the paper. "I mean, I like you. I just, crap, I don't know. I'm getting better about it. I think."

"Getting better at liking people?" she asks.

"Yeah. Something like that. Anyway, Chef is pretty amazing, he really knows his stuff."

"He makes terrible sfogliatelle," Amalea says smugly. She slaps another layer of butter onto it. And I'm no expert, but it seems a little extra forceful.

"Okay. Um, wow. Do you hate my teacher?" I smirk.

"I do not hate. Hate is a wasted emotion."

"Right. Well, I hate enough people for the both of us then. What's the deal? Do you want to talk about it? Were you lovers gone wrong?" Amalea looks up at me, her eyes wide with embarrassment. "Wait! Is he going to fail me because I'm staying with you? I guess he wouldn't, I don't even think we get graded—"

"Stop it! No, Davide will not fail you. He's a good man—"

"Davide, huh? How good is he?" I ask with a wink.

"Don't be stupid. Anyway, you drop it, I'll maybe teach you to make my famous sfogliatelle. You don't, I won't even let you taste a bite."

"Consider it dropped," I say smartly.

Amalea isn't ready to make good on her offer to teach me how to make the pastry, but she does let me sit in the kitchen and watch her make the labor intensive masterpiece.

"I've been meaning to ask you," I say. "How is your English so good?" I'm reaching for topics, but I really have been wondering. I assumed when I got here, I'd spend the entire month with everything lost in translation. Having Amalea as my host has really been a gift. "Do you have family in America or something?"

"No, no family. After…" Amalea tightens her apron and pauses, before rewording and starting again. "Several years ago, a couple from America moved to town. Carol was American, her husband, Benito was Italian. They came here to take care of his elderly parents, and Carol came to work in the store with me. She taught me to speak English." I feel like there's more to that story, but Amalea doesn't seem keen on sharing today, so I let it go.

"Is that a family recipe?" I ask, spreading a thick layer of creamy lardo onto a slice of fresh, rustic bread. If it weren't for Ben back home, I'm not sure I'd ever leave Spello. Or Amalea's kitchen. I take a bite and it's creamy in a way butter never could be and laced with rosemary and if I could marry a food this would be it.

"The sfogliatelle? *Si*. Passed down from my father's side. The lardo, no. Luca from next door brought that back from Modena this morning."

"It's delicious," I say, licking a glob off of my index finger.

"We will go one day. You and me. I know a man who makes *il pesto modenese* each morning. He will show you how."

"That sounds incredible. Maybe someday."

"You show more interest in the food than any of the other students I've had stay before."

"Really?"

Amalea nods and I can't help but feel a spark of pride ignite in myself for doing something right for a change.

"Did your mother cook with you a lot as a child? Is that why you have the appreciation of food?"

The flame has been blown out at the mention of my mom.

"Not really." I leave it vague, but Amalea looks up from the dough and stares at me, as if she's waiting for me to elaborate. "My mom and I were never really close. She has…*problems*."

"Ah," Amalea says. "Are things better now, that you are grown?"

"Not exactly. I don't live near her and my dad. And they are really involved with my youngest brother, so we don't connect a lot. But she's my mom…and I love her…and why am I talking about this when you threatened my life if I brought up Chef?"

Amalea cracks a small smile. "Fair enough."

She rounds the counter where she's been tirelessly rolling and stretching and layering the gorgeous dough, and reaches around me to open the freezer and place the plastic wrapped dough to chill. I have so much to learn from this woman.

"I wish I would've had a mom like you," I let the words slip out before I have a chance to consider them. How they must sound rude and creepy and strange from someone Amalea barely knows. "I mean, I wish I would have grown up with her teaching me to cook and stuff." I shrug, hoping I've managed to save things.

"*Sciocchezza*," Amalea says. "I'm sure your mother taught you many things."

I am not about to delve into the fact that my mom spent the majority of my childhood in rehab, running out on my dad and my brothers and I—leaving me to cook and get my brothers up for school. I'm not going to explain how my mom turned a blind eye to my dad's affair with our neighbor because she was too weak to do anything but look away. I won't admit that I hid so much of my life from my friends and from Ben back then because I was so embarrassed of how things really were, and could barely admit the realities to myself, much less tell anyone else. I don't say any of those things, but Amalea gives me a small nod, like she's transported herself into my brain and knows all the things.

"You should be thankful for your mother's faults."

"Excuse me?"

"A mother's job is to teach her children. You learned a valuable lesson from her. You learned exactly who you don't want to be."

I take another bite of the savory bread and consider this for a moment. I spent the better part of last year trying so hard to be nothing like my mother that I ended up spiraling out of control in signature Patricia MacPherson style.

"You remind me of my brother's pseudo-girlfriend," I say. Amalea raises her eyebrows at me. "In a good way! She always has these great little pieces of advice that, in her case, she probably read in a fortune cookie or under a bottle cap, but it's nice to, you know, talk to someone who can see things in a way that you can't. Shayna does that for me a lot."

"I'm glad I could help," Amalea says.

"Me too."

"And your boyfriend? Have you talked to him?" Amalea asks.

"Not as much as I'd like," I say. I've definitely called him more than he has called me, and our conversations are clipped and short, and not a whole lot is said. I don't want to brag about the amazing time I'm having when he's sitting at home alone. But our talks always end with an 'I love you,' so I guess I can't complain too much. "I don't know if it's him or me, or just the distance, but whenever we do talk, he seems short with me."

"Maybe he's just busy."

"Maybe." I lace my fingers together and try to choose my words in a way that won't leave me sounding like a jealous freak. "But he's off of school, and his boss is out of town so he's not working…" I think about all of the times he comes home late because he's out taking photos, and I just know that's how he's spending his time with me away. Hopefully he'll take enough that he won't sneak out the first night I'm home.

"Sometimes, it's easier to just accept the distance and anticipate the reunion," Amalea says. I don't know if that's right or wrong, but right now, it makes a lot of sense to me.

Eight

BEN

I'm pulling a delicious single serving of Salisburysteak and something that the frozen food company is trying to pass off as macaroni and cheese out of the microwave when my phone vibrates on the counter. It's not like I can't eat a proper meal without Quinn around, but why bother? It's just me, no point in messing up the entire kitchen.

"Hey, baby," I answer the phone and shut the microwave with my other hand.

"Hey, yourself. Long time no talk." Quinn's voice sounds the same, but it *feels* different. Like the distance and time change has crept its way into her words, softening the edges, making each word more meaningful, no matter what it is.

"I'm sorry. The time change is killer, you know?" I say it, but it's not the entire truth. Quinn is doing this amazing thing, and I'm happy for her. But part of me feels like she's figuring out just how much she's capable of—without me— and that maybe I just need to let her do that. She deserves it. She needs to realize just how freaking amazing she is for once without someone telling her. I know all of that, but the thought of it still terrifies the hell out of me. I want it for her, but selfishly, I don't want her to stop needing me. It's why I keep our conversations short. I don't want her worrying about me, or what's going on here, and it's just weird knowing that she's all the way over there, doing life changing things and I'm just…here. "What time is it there?"

Quinn yawns, "Just after three. I set an alarm so I could try to catch you when you got home. I've been getting pretty intimate with your voicemail, lately, so I figured I had to do something different."

"I'm glad you did," I say. Sometimes, the changes in Quinn catch me off guard. The Quinn I met in high school wouldn't have planned ahead like this. And she did it for me. Maybe my stupid-ass insecurities over her finding her own way are bullshit after-all.

"What are you doing?" she asks. I can picture her stretching out in the small room she described to me when we last talked. Alone.Bathed in gorgeous moonlight.

"Not a whole lot. Cleaning some lenses. Eating a bite," I say. I want to tell her about the offer on the photos, but I don't want to spoil any news she may have, or take away from it. I want her to have her moment.

"Ah, did you find some hot new thing to cook for you?" she says with a light laugh.

"Hardly," I say. "I've turned into a vegan since you left." I stir the noodles again, but still haven't brought myself to take a bite of them.

The line goes quiet. I can practically hear Italian crickets chirping on the other end.

"Ben," she says stoically. "You know we don't joke about serious things like that."

We both dissolve into hysterics, and I know that she's on the other side of the world wiping happy tears from her eyes, and that's all I need right now.

I remember some of the crazy things Quinn has gotten me to eat since I met her, and I'd take any one of them over this right now. Even those early dates where I think she was trying to get a rise out of me by getting me to eat things like sweet breads and burgers as big as my head. I did it because I was crazy about her and I loved that she challenged the hell out of me and never stopped surprising me.

And even from the other side of the world, when I can't stand to think about the space between us, she's surprising me. But I swear she needs me a little less every time we talk. She's finding that part of herself that her parents took away from her, and I just hope there's still room for me when she gets back.

The first time I ever considered texting Quinn. I tapped my thumb on the send button of my phone like I was doing Morse code, while I debated whether or not to go through with pressing it or not. It shouldn't have been that friggin' hard. In fact, it should've been nothing but straightforward. She was just a girl, and it was just a text message, right? She had told me to call her. So, why did her maybe-rejection cause me to have paralysis of the thumb? There was something about Quinn, though, that made different. She had me thinking she was such a hard ass at first, but I saw something else in her that first day at her house. Something I don't think she meant for me to see.

I was making it harder than it needed to be. Just needed to keep it simple. I deleted the message and started again.
 To: Quinn
 Hey, this is Ben. You free for lunch again today? My treat.
 Send.
 ####
"Okay, I'll bite, what the hell is this place?" I asked, as Quinn parallel parked her hybrid next to the rows of Harleys. I was stoked that she said yes to lunch, but hanging out with a biker gang wasn't exactly on my agenda.

"This place is to die for! I hope you're hungry!" Quinn said.

"I trust you." My lips stretched across my face into a nervous smile.

I motioned to the entrance, which happened to be a huge skull with bright orange hypnotizing eyes, where the gaping mouth serving as the entryway.

The sign above said, THE VORTEX.

"Well now, that's your first mistake," she said, adding an adorable wink. "It's not so bad inside, come on."

She grabbed my hand and pulled me through the bony face. I grazed my thumb over her soft ski, and wondered if she felt more than just my hand, if there was any possibility that she feltsomething more. I felt like a tool admitting to myself that I already did.

Once inside, The Vortex was a lot less intimidating. It honestly couldhave easily passed for a small Applebee's. The walls were full of tchotchkes like old street signs, barber's poles and all sorts of other kitsch. It's was already past the normal lunch hour, so the majority of the tables were empty. Quinn walked right past the hostess stand and pulled me in the direction of the patio. She decided on a table right in front of a mural of a fire-breathing skull with pin-up style devils lounging across it. So much for the Americana theme.

"So, what's good here?" I opened my menu and glanced up at Quinn. She quickly diverted her eyes, but I did catch her staring at my arms as she unrolled her silverware and smoothed the paper napkin onto her lap.

"You won't need that," she said. "I'll order for you." She plucked the menu out of my hands and set it on top of hers at the edge of the table.

"Okay, a little controlling, but I like it," I said.

She flipped her long brown hair over her shoulder and leaned back in her chair.

"Ha, yeah, I guess I am." She smiled at me, and it struck me for the first time just how completely out of my league she was.

"That's fine. But you should know when ordering, that I'm a strict vegetarian."

Quinn's smile transformed into tightly pursed lips and her brow furrowed. "Wait, seriously?"

"No way, are you kidding? Bacon and I have a very deep love affair going."

"Oh thank god. That right there would've been a deal breaker for sure," she said with a laugh. "Wait, I mean, not like this is anything..."

I nodded. "Right."

Quinn picked up one of the menus again and stared down at it.

"At least not yet. I give it a week," I said.

"A week before what?" she asked.

"A week before you're begging me to go out with you," I said. I linked my fingers behind my head and leaned back in my chair. I was hoping that the arrogant smirk on my face would camouflage my nervousness.

"Is that right?" She raised one eyebrow and grinned.

"I'm counting on it."

"You've got your work cut out for you then, I'm sort of an emotional cripple," she said. Hurt flashed across her eyes, before the forced smile masked it. And I knew in that second that I wanted to know her more. I wanted to know where that flash of pain came from, and how to take it away. I wanted to make it better. In that brief moment of vulnerability, I knew she was a girl I could love. That I wanted to love, and I held my breath waiting to see what she'd say next, because I wasn't sure I had words.

The waiter, M-A-Double-X, according to his nametag, had perfect timing, and I motioned for Quinn to go ahead with her order.

"Okay, I'm gonna have the Spanish Fly Burger," she said. I raised a curious eyebrow at the name. What the hell had I gotten myself into?

"What can I get you?" Maxx asked me, but his eyes were still locked on Quinn's.

"He'll have the Double Bypass Burger," Quinn interjected.

Maxx made a mental note of it, smiled at Quinn once more, and walked away.

"Double Bypass? Seriously?"

Quinn nodded with a wicked grin. "Seriously."

"My great-aunt just died during heart surgery," I said.

Quinn eyes grew wide and she chomped down on her straws. Two of them. "Crap—"

"I'm kidding. Lighten up, woman," I said as I cracked a smile.

Quinn reached across the table and swatted at my arm. "You're an ass!"

"I've been called worse once or twice."

The Double Bypass Burger, it turned out, was loaded with more cheese, fried eggs and bacon than a breakfast buffet, and was served between two grilled cheese sandwiches in place of hamburger buns, and I ate until I wasn't sure how I was going to dislodge myself from the tiny metal chair and cram myself back into Quinn's tiny car.

"So, thank you for lunch," she said. She pulled her car into the space next to mine back in the school parking lot.

"Absolutely. Hey, if you don't have plans tomorrow, we can do it again—"

She checked her watch and cut me off. "Crap! Carter! I'm sorry, I completely forgot, I've got to go!"

I reached for the door handle, suddenly unable to remove myself from her car fast enough. "Oh, okay."

Carter? I should've known we were in the friend zone, but for some reason, I failed to pick up on that vibe back at the restaurant.

"My brother, Carter, I'm supposed to meet him at the airport. He's in from Stanford."

"Gotcha," I said, and my relief was palpable.

"But really, I'd like to hang out again, I had a great time."

"Even for an emotional cripple?"

She smirked shyly, and I saw a whole different side of her in that single expression. I changed my mind from back at the restaurant—this was the face I would have done anything to get to know more of.

"Absolutely," I said.

"So, what's been going on?"

"So much. For starters, the woman that I'm staying with, Amalea, she's just…I can't even tell you, Ben. She's amazing. She took me to this coastal town and this man on the side of the road, he taught me how to make pesto! Not like the crappy kind I make at home where I would always put too much oil, this was something special. Anyway, he taught me right there, on the *street*. And Amalea, she promised she'd show me how to make her famous sfogliatelle before I leave. She's never shown anyone outside of her family, but she trusts me. Me! With the recipe." Even through the phone, across time zones and thousands of miles, I can feel Quinn glowing in the way that she does when she is genuinely excited about something.

"It sounds incredible," I say. I take a bite of my less-than-mediocre microwavable dinner and try to imagine what she's experiencing.

"I wish you could be here to see it all."

"Me—" There's a knock at the door. "Hang on, baby. Come in!" I call.

The knob turns and Carter peers around the half-open door. "Hey, buddy, Shayna and I are on our way out of town. Last chance to tag along."

I cover the phone. "No thanks, man, I'll be fine here."

"Is that Carter?" Quinn asks on the other end of the phone.

"Yep," I confirm.

"Tell him I said hi," she says.

"Your sister says hello," I say.

Carter smiles and yells, "Merry Christmas, Quinnlette. Love you!" He turns his attention back to me. "You good then, man?" I nod and he backs out of the door and closes it behind him.

"Still haven't changed your mind about going home?" Quinn asks.

"I *am* home. And you'll be home soon."

"That is true," Quinn agrees with a laugh. "We should plan something for New Year's Eve. I get in the day before."

"Definitely. I'll figure something out," I say. "But you need to get some sleep, baby."

Quinn yawns deeply in response. "You're right. I miss you."

"You too. Love you, baby."

I end the call and then toss my dinner into the garbage. I'm not depressed, exactly. I'm just feeling pretty damn useless right now. And maybe I even regret not going home. A little. I don't even know if I'd be welcome there, but sinking into the sofa in this empty house, it gets me that this is the first holiday that I've ever spent completely alone. Right now, I'd almost welcome the sight of my mom's precision wrapped presents and strict holiday schedule. *Just something* to take up some space in the hollow feeling spreading inside me. Normally I dig the independence, but right now, independence feels a lot like loneliness.

Nine

BEN

My phone buzzing on my nightstand wakes me up from a deep sleep.

"What'd you forget?" I answer assuming it's Quinn.

"Ben?" Caroline's voice is completely unchanged from the last time I heard it. Or, since the day I met her, sophomore year, when we were just kids. And it's the familiarity of her voice and sweet southern twang that feels so good right now, it's like hearing your home language in a foreign country.

I rub my palm across my cheek. "Linney? Wow, it's been a long time."

Three beats pass before either one of us says anything more. Just seconds, but long enough for my mind to go all sorts of directions trying to figure out what it is that Caroline and I have to talk about at this hour, and something else inside me is so glad that she called, because at least that means someone needs something from me, even if it's just a sympathetic ear.

"I know. I'm sorry to bother you. Can you talk?"

Can I isn't the right question. *Should I* is a better one. Caroline has been calling for weeks, and I owe her a return phone call. After all the years we've known each other, to not show her the respect of answering her calls has been a total dick move.

"Absolutely, is everything okay?"

"Sort of. Not really," Caroline stumbles over each word. "I mean, it is now."

"Linney, what's going on?" There's something about her voice that makes me think this is much bigger than a bad day or a call to say she misses me.

"I've been trying to get ahold of you for a couple of weeks now. I didn't know what to say on a message. Did you see my calls?"

"No, sorry," I lie.

"Right. I just…"

I stretch my arm across the bed to hit the lamp on the table. "Linney, you can talk to me." It's never been this hard to pull words out of her. We always had the communication thing down.

"I know, it's just weird now, I know you're living with Quinn…"

Caroline mentioning Quinn's name makes me pause. "I am," I say.

"Is she there? Quinn, I mean."

"No, no. She's out of town for school. Why?"

"No reason. I just didn't figure she'd be thrilled with you talking with me. I didn't want to get you into trouble or anything."

"Don't worry about that, Linney. Quinn and I are doing great." Even though she's halfway around the world, and doesn't really seem to need me the way she used to.

"Good. Okay. Glad to hear it." Her words are short like she's so distracted she's trying to sound coherent.

"What's going on? Caroline. Talk to me." I readjust the pillow under me, still in a bit of a haze after being woken up.

"When was the last time you talked to your parents?"

I pull in a quick breath. "It's been a while." Did they put her up to this?

"Okay, so, this is probably really weird, but I was calling because I didn't know if you'd be coming to see them for Christmas or not—"

"No, I'm not. What does that have to do with anything?" They definitely put her up to this. Mom couldn't bother calling and inviting me herself, she was likely worried I'd show up with Quinn if I came home.

"I'm living with them. I mean, they've invited me to live with them for a while, and I moved in last month."

"What? I don't understand, how did that come about?"

"It's a really long story. Basically, I needed somewhere safe to go, and my mom talked to your mom, who really misses you, by the way, we all do, really—"

"Wait, back up. Somewhere safe? Are you okay, Linney?" I'm now wide awake, sitting up in bed, heart slamming inside my chest. I feel like an asshole of a friend for ignoring her calls.

"I am now, like I said. Things just got a little crazy back home, and I needed to go somewhere new for a while. I hope I'm doing the right thing, I don't even know anymore…"

"And you're there, at my parent's house now?"

"Yeah," she says.

"I've got to let you go," I say. I hoist myself out of bed and grab a pair of jeans and a wrinkled t-shirt off of the floor.

"Ben, I'm sorry. Does that upset you? Crap." She sounds embarrassed, and that's the last thing I want.

"No, no, it's nothing like that. I just, I need to see if I can still get a flight out. I'm coming home." I let the words tumble out of my mouth before I have the chance to think them through. I don't pause to consider them as I pack, or as I fork over what little available credit I have on my credit card, or as I board the plane, or as I step onto the brick walkway that leads up to my parents' house.

Because if I stopped to think about it, I might realize that this may not be the best idea I've ever had.

Because if I think too long about what I'm doing, I might lose sight of the one thing that is clearer than anything right now—and that's that Linney needs someone.

Linney needs *me*.

~~~~~~~~~~~~~~~~

Even though I'm exhausted, I take the steps up to the house two at a time, because, really, what's the point in postponing the inevitable awkwardness? But once I reach the door, I'm not sure what to do. Do I knock? I still have a key, but I can't just let myself in, can I? *Shit.*

The front door swings open and my dad stands there, eyes wide, jaw slack.

"Ben?" He says, as if he doesn't recognize me, or can't believe I'm really standing here. It's only been a year, I haven't changed. I mean, I have. Of course. But not in any way that counts. Right?

"What are you doing here, son?" He pulls me in for a hug. I don't remember the last time he did that, and it's awkward because it's been so long, and because he's my dad but I tower over him. I sort of had this vision that when I saw my parents, they'd be different. My stupid ego sort of let me think that they'd upset about me leaving, that they'd be frail or something ridiculous. But they're not, because Dad, at least, looks good. Healthy. He smiles broadly and I can't help but feel glad to be here, even if that nagging voice in the back of my head tells me it's wrong.

"Hey, Pop," I say. He pulls me in through the door and, though I notice that the exterior of the house has been painted a light gray rather than the taupe it was before and the stones leading up to the house have been replaced, inside, it feels like time has stood still. The photos on the walls are the same, a shot of me for every year I was in school, lined up with precision. The only thing that feels the least bit different is the scale. Everything seems a little smaller. The sofa not quite so overstuffed. The fireplace mantel not quite so high. It's not because I've grown, I guess my perception has just changed. Maybe that's what happens when you move away.

My dad stands across from me, staring. Smiling. "Couldn't miss another holiday with us, couldya?" he asks.

"Something like that," I say, grinning back at him.

"Well, we're glad you're here, son. Wish you would have called, I could have picked you up from the airport," Dad says.

I shrug. "I didn't want to put anyone out. I've got a rental." Also, I didn't know how long I'd be staying, or if shit would hit the fan as soon as I walked through the door, and I'd have to turn right back around and leave.

"How was your Thanksgiving? We missed hearing from you," Dad says.

"Missed you too, Pop. It was good. Quinn cooked a big meal, all the trimmings." I beam with pride.

"Good. Still wish you would have been here, though. Nothing like your mom's cooking."

I smile to oblige him. "Hey, is Ma around?"

Dad's smile turns downward. "She is, yeah. She's in the basement with…" He lets his gaze drift around the room.

"With Caroline?" I ask. He raises his eyebrows, looking relieved that I already know.

"Yep. Just getting a few things set up down there for her. You could head on down, or you can wait up here with your old man."

"Yeah, that's fine, I'll just wait," I say. Dad takes a seat in his recliner and I follow suit, sitting on the sofa. "So, listen, what's going on with Linney?"

Dad rubs his palms together and sighs. "I don't know the whole story, Ben, and what I do know probably isn't for me to tell. I'm sure she'll tell you everything when she's ready."

"But, she's okay, right?"

"I think she'll be glad you're here. She could use a friend," Dad says.

"That's exactly why I'm here." So fast. Without thinking about anything but being here. And I know there are consequences to this decision that I haven't even begun to piece together yet, but I'm pushing those thoughts away until I get a chance to *do* something here. Hopefully something good. Something that makes a difference. Or, maybe that's just my arrogance thinking I have anything left to offer. Maybe I've done my fixing and now it's over.

"You really came. Wow. I didn't mention it to you, Mr. and Mrs. Shaw because I really didn't think you were serious, Ben!" Caroline rushes to me from the doorway and falls into my arms. I kiss the top of her head and breathe in the familiar smell of honey from her hair.

Caroline looks the same. Same blond hair, long down her back. Same warm blush on her pale skin when she smiles at me. Oh, shit, was that friendly greeting out of bounds? It's the first time I've let the question of how Quinn would react if she were here cross my mind.

I want to talk to Linney. I want to find out what made her leave Kentucky, her school, her friends, her parents. How it is that she ended up living in my parents basement. If someone hurt her and I need to hunt them down and beat the ever-loving shit out of them. But as I pull back, away from Caroline, I see my mom standing at the top of the stairs that lead up from the basement.

"We should give you a minute," Caroline says, clasping her hands together and backing into the kitchen with my dad following close behind. "It's good to see you, though, Ben." She flashes me one last smile before disappearing into the kitchen.

"Benjamin," Mom says. Her mouth forms a tight line and I feel like I'm twelve years old all over again.

"How you doing, Ma?" I ask.

"You came for Christmas?" she asks. She peers around me, then out the window for a split second.

"I did. And to check on Linney."

"Of course," she says. "That's nice of you. Guess I did something right raising you."

"Ma…" She's hit the ground running with her passive-aggressive remarks. I eye my small duffel bag that I dropped in the corner, debating how shitty it'd look it I picked up my crap and went back to LA right now. This couldn't get any more uncomfortable than it is. At the same time I'm pondering that, my mom is looking out the window again, and it finally dawns on me what she's doing. "She isn't here, Ma. It's just me."

I see her shoulders fall, visibly relaxing at the news that Quinn didn't make the trip with me, and it pisses me off.

"Well, that's a Christmas gift in itself," she says under her breath.

"I heard that. I can go, if you'd like." I motion to the door. I mean it. I'll happily grab my bag and leave now. Well, after I find out what's wrong with Linney. And maybe Mom knows that. That I came for a reason, and I won't leave until I've figured out what's going on with Linney.

"Don't leave," Mom says. She absently runs her hand along the back of the sofa. "Are you two…broken up?"

"No," I say, feeling anger bubble up and percolate in my chest. "Not at all."

The disappointment on Mom's face couldn't be more clear if it were scrawled out in permanent marker or flashing on a neon sign.

"Quinn's away. In Europe. For school."

"Hmm," Mom utters a non-committal, unimpressed noise. "But you're here. And you'll be staying here for the holiday?"

"If that's alright"

"Of course, Benny," she says. I cringe at the nickname, but she waves me over for a hug and I'm glad the initial shit-storm is over with. "We can talk about things after you settle in. Oh! And Caroline mentioned some shopping she needed to get done. Maybe you can take her into town?"

"Sure thing, Ma."

Surely Quinn wouldn't fault me for taking off with Caroline if it meant getting away from my mom.

Ten

QUINN

I need help lugging the old cookbooks that Chef agreed to give me rather than throwing them out back to Amalea's place. They're heavy and will probably cost every cent I have to my name to get back to the States, but I need them. So, Chef Baldassare helps carry them up the hill and into the house. I push the heavy door open and he and I both drop the books onto the solid wood table with a huff when Amalea walks in.

"Mi scusi," Amalea says. Her hand goes to her chest at the sight of Davide, and her face contorts into an expression that I haven't yet seen on her. Her full, red mouth is usually grinning about something, whether it's a good glass of wine, licking the spoon after mixing a bowl of cannoli cream, or chatting with a customer in her shop. But right now, her lips purse and eyes squint and it's either anger or confusion or surprise, or hell, maybe all of those things in one. But there's definitely something in her almond eyes that screams there's something more between she and Davide.

I stare up at the raw, exposed beams in the ceiling rather than look directly at Amalea. I wonder if I screwed up royally by bringing Chef here with me.

"Lea," he says, dipping his head politely. His voice is different than it is in class. It's transformed from the authoritative, masculine bark, to something smooth and warm like a glass of amaretto. So much so that I cut my eyes away from ceiling-gazing to double check that Davide is still the man standing in the room. It is him, greeting Amalea with that nickname in that low, sexy voice.

Amalea wipes her hands on the yellow kitchen towel and tosses it absently onto the counter top, which, from what I've observed of Amalea in my short stay, is highly unusual. She isn't freakishly organized like Ben's mom, but she keeps things neat, especially in the kitchen. Amalea extends her graceful hand in an even more unusual gesture—since from the day that I met her, I've only seen her do the whole double-kiss-on-the-cheeks bit with people that Europeans are so found of.

Chef ignores her outstretched hand, puts his hands on each of her upper arms and pulls her in, lightly kissing each of her cheeks. Like a boss.

"Davide," she replies breathlessly. "It's been a long time. A very long time."

He gives her a simple, quick nod, but his eyes convey something much more meaningful and intimate.

Holy shit, this is like something out of a romance novel and I feel like a total creeptastic voyeur standing right smack in the middle of their moment.

"I should go…call Ben…" I say. I begin backing out of the room, but Amalea holds a palm up to stop me.

"Don't rush off, Davide was just leaving." Her eyes don't leave his as she says the words. The spark in his dark eyes fades and his brow furrows in disappointment.

But Chef doesn't wait to be told twice.He grabs his coat off of the back of the wooden chair with the peeling blue paint and walks out the door.

"Thanks for helping with the books!" I call after him, but he's already too far to hear me.

"Did you ask him to come here?" Amalea turns to me and asks. Her cheeks are that rare shade of scarlet, reserved only for the most embarrassing or infuriating times. I hate that I caused either. Or, possibly, both.

"He was just helping me bring those cookbooks in." I motion to the normally clear table, now littered with books."I couldn't carry them all by myself. I'm sorry?"

Amalea waves me off. *"Figurati!"*

"Sorry," I repeat, not knowing if she's told me to fuck off or not to worry about it.

"I need a drink." She opens the small white cabinet above the tiny stove and pulls down a clear bottle with a purple flower on it. She pours two small glasses of the liquid from the pretty bottle and sets one down in front of me before throwing the other back in one quick gulp. It isn't the dainty, ladylike sips she normally takes of her liquor.

"Cheers?" I mutter.

I wrap my lips around the small glass and pour the liquid down into my throat. I try to fight the outward cringe, not knowing if this small glass of alcohol cost as much as my rent or not. But it's hard. How can something that was in such nice packaging taste like such complete ass? I struggle not to gag or shake like my body is desperate to do as the liquid singes my throat and burns all the way down into my stomach.

"You want another?" Amalea asks.

"No," I croak out, like a fifteen-year-old who has just taken her first swig of skunk beer. "What is that?"

"Grappa," she says. Amalea cuts several large chunks off of a massive wheel of Parmigiano-Reggiano cheese and pops a piece into her mouth. I follow suit and am so relieved to have the salty deliciousness get to work dissolving the jet fuel aftertaste of the Grappa in my mouth.

She frantically starts pulling food out of the refrigerator, the pantry, and cupboards. She slices cheeses, shaves different salamis, and prosciutto and spreads black and white truffle butter onto fresh bread.

"What are we celebrating?" I ask, admiring the incredible spread.

Amalea pours herself another shot and downs it quickly. It must be an acquired taste.

"I survived seeing Davide," she says. She's normally the picture of poise and calm. But right now, Amalea looks a little wild.

"What do you mean, survived? Did I screw up royally by bringing him here? I'm so sorry."

She shakes her head. "It's a good thing. It needed to happen, and better with you here than me all alone."

I don't press her any further, but she continues on her own.

"Davide and I used to be lovers," she says, rolling the small, empty glass back and forth in her palm. *I could have guessed that*, I want to say. Still, I'm a little stunned by the candid admission.

"He seems like a pretty good catch." I swipe a piece of cheese and dry salami while the conversation is still light—before I look like a complete jerk for eating while she spills her guts. I envy the children that Davide and Amalea could have produced together. The amazing family-style meals that would be an everyday staple in that home make my mouth water just imagining them.

"He was. *Is*. He should be happy." She tosses her long, dark hair back over her shoulder.

"Amalea, what happened? I mean, you're a total fox. He had to be a complete moron to let you get away. And here I had him pegged for a good guy." I shake my head and cram the last bite of cheese into my mouth. Okay, the second to last one. I reach over and grab another chunk of the soft, sweet cheese. The flavors are so much more complex than I expected from a piece of cheese. It's absolutely delicious.

"It's Caciotta. Sheep's cheese. Good, no?" Amalea stops to say.

"It's incredible."

Amalea sighs. "Davide *is* a good man. I was the one who ruined things."

A girl after my own heart.

"Come on, you're adorable, and you can cook better than anyone I've ever met. Even Chef." I say with a wink.

"I was having an affair," Amalea deadpans.

"Oh, shizz, you were cheating on Davide?" *Classy, Quinn,* I mentally scold myself.

Amalea shakes her head and looks so much more than ashamed.

"I was married. I was having an affair *with* Davide. My husband was also a good man. He gave me this home. He worked hard. But I loved Davide from the first day I saw him." She re-ties the belt on her floral print dress, cinching the waist tightly. "My friend, the American, Carol? After I started seeing Davide, Carol began teaching me English so that she and I could communicate about it without Enzo understanding. It was callous and cruel. But I was stupid. And selfish. And so in love with Davide. I couldn't see anything outside of him."

"But your husband, Enzo, he found out?"

Amalea shakes her head and stares down at her hands. "He never found out. I was supposed to be home when he came home from work. I was, every other night. We ate dinner at the same hour every single night. But I wasn't. I had left the shop early to take siesta at Davide's."

I'm not entirely certain where this is going, but I know it's not going to go well based on the low, sullen tone of Amalea's voice. I reach over for the bottle of grappa and refill both of our glasses. Amalea grasps hers, but doesn't drink it.

"My husband, Enzo, he was worried because I wasn't here. He went to check the shop, and I wasn't there either. I'd fallen asleep at Davide's, after we…"

I take the opportunity to gulp my glass of jet fuel, this time, knowing well enough to have the bite of parmesan ready to dull the flame.

I clear my throat. "I get the point."

"I woke up at Davide's house and it was dark, I knew Enzo would be out looking for me. By the time I got home, the *Polizia* were already here."

"Fuck," I say. The word slips out, while imaging Amalea running in the front door after her tryst with another man to find the cops in her home. "*Mi scusi.*" I apologize.

Amalea nods. "Enzo was hit by a car and passed on."

"So, you broke it off with Davide…because of what happened with Enzo."

"The guilt, how could I ever look at Davide again, knowing that it was my fault?"

"But it wasn't," I say. "It wasn't either one of your faults. I mean, you didn't set out to hurt anyone."

"No, but unintentional hurt doesn't make it any less wrong."

"So, what, you're going to spend the rest of your life holed up in here, eating all of this food and working at your little store…actually that doesn't sound half bad." I laugh and it makes Amalea laugh and it almost disguises the tiny tears in the corners of her eyes.

She reaches over and covers my hand with hers. "You're a good girl, Quinn. I'm glad you came."

"I am, too." She may be the first person to ever tell me that. "When was the last time you saw Davide?"

Amalea looks up at the ceiling, like she's calculating. "I've seen him around town, at the market, the train station…but I haven't seen him this close in…five years."

"Five years?" I think about how I'm missing Ben and I've only been away from him for a few weeks. I can't imagine how my heart would ache being away from him for years. Or worse, as close as Amalea and Davide are, but not being able to communicate. "Amalea, you need to fix this! Five years?"

"There's nothing left to fix. What was between Davide and I is broken. Gone."

"It's not. Trust me. I've been there—"

"Quinn, you're lovely, but you're just a girl, this is beyond your ability to relate."

"I don't think so." And so I tell her. I tell her how I met Ben that summer, how I fell so insanely, ridiculously hard for him, but it scared the shit out of me. I tell her all the ways I tried to push him away because the words I love you scared me more than any monster ever could. I avoided looking her in the eye when I told her I got angry with Ben for not sticking up to his parents when they invited Caroline to stay with them while she looked at colleges. And how I took that anger, and went over to Mark's house and let him strip me down and slept with him on his sofa, intent on getting back at Ben—or just feeling anything other than the searing hurt.

And I told her how Ben tried so hard to forgive me, but I wouldn't let him. Because hanging on to my guilt was the punishment I'd given myself. And back then, I would have rather be miserable than happy. But Ben eventually proved to me that love could withstand the fuck-ups, if you tried hard enough.

"I know it's not the same situation, but trust me, nothing is ever too broken if you love him. And by the way he looked at you, I'm positive he still has those feelings for you, Amalea."

She pulls me in tightly, smothering me with her own sobs and tears and for once, I'm the one comforting someone else, rather than the one needing to be consoled.

Eleven

BEN

It feels strange to be back in Atlanta, especially with Caroline in the passenger seat of the car—Dad's sensible sedan.

Caroline fidgets in the seat, twisting her hair, tapping her foot. I don't know if I'm making her uncomfortable, or if it's whatever is going on in her life that forced her to move to a different state that's working her nerves.

"You alright over there?" I ask.

"Yep," is all that Caroline replies.

I haven't pressed for any more information about what's going on with her. *Yet.* I keep trying to say something to her, to ask why she's suddenly living in my parents' basement, but I feel like I'd be overstepping. She is the one who tracked me down, calling in the middle of the night, though, so she must *want* to talk about it, right?

"Good. So, where to?"

She lets out a small sigh, "I don't really know. I don't know where anything is around here. But I need to get my mom and dad a Christmas gift. It'll be late, but I need to send them something, you know? And maybe we could get some lunch? Your mom keeps trying to cook for me, but I don't want her to have to do that. And honestly, I'm kind of scared to touch anything in the kitchen. It's all so…perfect."

"Sure," I say. "And trust me, I know what you mean." I visualize the drawer dividers in my mom's kitchen. Perfectly spaced. Color coordinated. And don't you dare put a plastic spatula in with the wooden ones. Poor Caroline is in for a treat living with my parents. They've always liked her, and she gets along with them, but *living* with them? That's a different story entirely. "How about we hit the mall, then we'll grab something to eat on that end of town?" I ask.

I start to steer the car toward the mall, but instead, at the last second, decide to go the opposite direction.

It finally dawns on me that Carter and Shayna are here, in Atlanta, too. They left only a few hours before me. It's not a crime for me to be here, but I sure as shit don't want them to see me here with Caroline before I have the chance to tell Quinn what's going on. "Hey, tell you what. The mall is going to be madness today, but there's this really cool strip of shops on the other end of the city, you game?"

Caroline shrugs, very non-committal. "Whatever is fine." And I'm sort of wondering why I hopped my ass on the first plane out town when she's acting the way that she is. But there's got to be more to it than she's letting on. I just have to give her a chance to tell me.

She tangles her fingers together, pulls them apart, and pats her knees—anything but just remaining still. I reach over and cover her hands with mine to calm her movements. It instantly does the trick, I feel her hands stop and her body relaxes. As if a switch has been flipped. And I'd be lying if I said that knowing that I did that for her didn't feel damn good.

"It's good to see you, Linney," I say.

I really look at her for the first time since I got here. She looks the same as always. She's going to be one of those women that age really well, just like her mom. But her eyes look different. Worried. Uneasy. Maybe a little broken.

"So, are you going to tell me what's going on?" I finally ask. "I mean, you moved in with my parents of all people, it had to be pretty serious." It's my lame attempt at a joke that neither one of us bothers to laugh at.

"Your parents aren't bad, Ben."

"Yeah, well, neither are yours," I say. "So why leave them?"

"Your mom was so happy to see you," she says.

"Stellar job changing the subject, Linney." I wink at her. I don't press, though, because Linney has never had a problem talking to me so I know she will when she's ready. And I'll be here when she is.

I pull into a parking spot in the Little Five Points district and rush around the car to open Linney's door for her.

"Some things never change, Ben," she says, smiling at the gesture.

"Like what?"

"Like the fact that you are, and have always been, the biggest gentlemen I know."

"Guess Ma raised me right," I say with a goofy smile, remembering Mom's comment back at the house. "No big deal."

Linney stops in the middle of the crosswalk and looks up at me. "You have no idea what a big deal it is, Ben."

I don't know how to respond to that, so I just put my hand on her back and lead the rest of the way across the street. I feel like she's trying to tell me something that I'm just too freaking dense to get.

"Tell you what, I've been up all night and I haven't eaten since breakfast yesterday, well, unless you count two bites of

Salisbury steak. Anyway, what do you think about getting lunch first?"

"Fine by me."

We decide on Fellini's because the pizza is good, and Quinn and I have never eaten there together, and I feel like if I can avoid places that I've been with Quinn, maybe I won't feel like such an asshole about being here without telling.

"You want to find us a table and I'll order the pizza?" I ask.

"Table or booth?" Caroline says, grabbing plastic forks and napkins from the edge of the counter. "Wait," she says, tapping a fork on my forearm. "You always prefer a table so you have more leg—"

"Well, hey there." The voice rings in my ears and I can't help the instantaneous hope that I've imagined it.

I turn away from the counter, toward the voice. But it's not in my head. It's real.

Shayna and Carter are standing three feet away from Caroline and I.

"Hey," I reply.

Carter has his arms crossed over his chest, and the normally laid-back vibe he exudes has evaporated. He always shakes my hand when he sees me. I mock him about it, because I imagine that he does it all day long in the office when he greets clients. But he doesn't uncross his arms to reach for my hand this time. And I know it's because of me. I guess I should expect that: he's close and protective of Quinn. He and I have always had that in common.

"I thought you said you weren't going to make it home? Change of plans?" Carter asks.

Fuck.

"Yeah, decided to come see my folks after all."

Shayna scoffs. "Does Quinn know that?"

She's looking directly at Caroline when she asks. And I can't help but worry about Caroline even more right now, because, unlike Shayna, confrontation is not Linney's strong suit on a good day, and whatever she's going through right now has definitely made her even more timid.

"No, no, not yet. Last minute thing, you know?"

"Right," Shayna says, puckering her mouth like she's tasted something sour.

"So, do you guys want to eat with us?" I ask. Caroline raises her eyebrows, silently questioning whether that's a good idea or not.

"No, man, thanks. We just ate. We've got to get over to Shayna's parents' house. How long will you be in town?" Carter asks.

My relief is palpable that they're on their way out. "Just a few days. Got to get back to work as soon as Ron gets back into town." *And I sold some of my work.* But I can't even tell him that. I haven't even told Quinn. What the hell am I doing?

"Yeah. And Quinn will be home soon," Shayna interjects, cocking her head to one side. As if I hadn't already been counting down the days.

"Can't wait," I say. "Merry Christmas, guys."

"Merry Christmas," Shayna says. "Oh, and hey, I didn't catch your name?" Shayna turns to Linney, her face full of suspicion masked with a smile.

"Caroline," Linney answers and extends her hand.

"Right. Should have guessed." Shayna looks at Carter with her mouth agape, then back at me and shakes her head before they leave the restaurant together.

Fuck.

Carter reappears just as I'm walking to the table with our food. He leans in a little too close, his tone a little too sharp, that for a minute, I forget that we live down the hall from each other, that I consider him a friend.

"I'm not going to ruin Quinn's trip by telling her I saw you here today. It doesn't mean I think it's okay. Are we clear?"

"Carter—" I start to explain, but really, I have no defense. So I just thank him, which is probably just as bad.

Why didn't I at least call Quinn on the drive to my parents' house from the airport? I answer my own question as soon as it pops into my head. Because the last time I called Quinn and told her that Linney was coming to stay with my parents, she turned around and screwed some other guy. And now she's a world away. I can't even consider the consequences in this situation. *But she's a different Quinn.* But not different enough that me being out with Linney wouldn't cause…Fuck, I can't even think about it.

What am I doing here? Putting everything on the line with Quinn like this? Shayna will probably call Quinn the second she walks out the door.

Fuck. Fuck. Fuck.

I slide the tray of pizza across the table top. Seeing Carter and Shayna has effectively suppressed my appetite.

"I gather you didn't tell Quinn you were coming?" Caroline asks, spreading her napkin neatly out on her lap.

"No, I hadn't had a chance. That was her brother and his girlfriend, if you didn't catch that. I guess it won't be long before she knows."

"Do you want to call her?" Caroline asks.

"I probably should, but honestly, I don't want to mess up what she has going right now. And I hope Carter has the same idea." Please let him have the same idea.

"I'm sorry," she says, lowering her head.

"Don't be. You didn't ask me to come, I didit because I wanted to." And for that, maybe now she'll talk to me.

"But why?"

"Because we're friends, Linney. And you sounded like you could use one on the phone."

Linney takes a small bite of her pizza and chews slowly.

She swallows, wipes her hands and then speaks again. "Aren't you going to ask me what's wrong?"

"Only if you're ready to tell me."

"I guess I sort of have to, being as I just screwed up your relationship. Again." She runs her fingertip along the rim of her glass and watches me. Her look is a little too intense.

I scoff, trying to lighten the mood. "You didn't screw anything up."

Caroline looks slightly relieved. "Where is Quinn, anyway?"

"Italy. A program for culinary school."

"Wow, that's impressive."

"It's pretty cool. She's been really worked hard, and she loves what she does. She's doing really great." At least I assume she is. I keep our conversations so short. At least that way, I don't have to feel a pang of disappointment if she doesn't say how much she misses me.

"But how are you doing…like together? I mean, you did come out here…"

"Linney, don't read more into it than it is. Quinn and I are great. She's amazing."

"Nice. Good," Caroline says nodding.

"Plus, it's Christmas, and I sort of have some stuff to work out with my folks."

"Yeah, it sounds like it. What's up with all of that anyway?"

I run my hand along the table top and consider my words carefully. I don't want to talk bad about my family, but the situation is what it is. "Mom gave me an ultimatum. Them or Quinn. In my mind, the one that gives you the ultimatum is the one that loses you. Simple."

"No it's not, Ben. Not as close as you and your family are."

"Were," I interject.

"The thing is, Quinn never did a single thing to them."

"But she hurt you." Linney reaches across the table and rubs my arm. It's a simple touch, nothing more than I've done to her since I've been back in town, but it *feels* different. It *feels* like maybe Quinn might have been right all of the times she said Caroline was still after more than just a friendship with me.

"And I've hurt her, too," I qualify. I'm hurting her right now by being here. So why am I doing it? I try to be nonchalant when I pull my arm away and grab the tent-shaped desert menu off of the end of the table, and stare at it harder than I really need to.

Caroline shifts in her chair. "Is she—"

I don't even let her finish whatever question she's about to ask.

"Linney, listen, I know you mean well, I do. But I really don't want to talk about Quinn," I say. "With you."

"Of course. I understand," she says. Her lips form a tight, irritated line and she has a look of anything but understanding.

"Do you want to leave?" she asks. Her eyes glisten with what might be tears forming and the last thing I want to do is leave and spend the next half-hour in the car apologizing for upsetting her more than she already was when I got here. No, maybe I can turn this around. Change the subject.

"No, let's stay and eat."

Caroline purses her lips and gives a quick bob of her head.

There's a pause that stretches into a lengthy, awkward silence. I flew all the way out here thinking that I could do some good. But things with Linney feel strained, like she's looking for something more than I can offer her. She and I could always talk, but since I got here, it feels like she wants to focus on Quinn, and I can't do that. Not right now. Not when I know I'm totally fucking things up with her by being here.

"How's school? I mean, what are you going to do now that you're out here? How long are you staying?"

"I'm not sure, honestly. It was a quick move. My mom panicked and didn't know what to do with me, so she made arrangements to have me stay with your family...and...here I am. I don't know if I'm supposed to enroll in school here...or if this is just a temporary move... I guess I'll just wait to hear what Mom and Dad say."

"They aren't coming in for Christmas?"

Linney shakes her head and swirls the straw in her drink around some more.

"No, dad couldn't take any more time off of work. He's missed a lot lately with...everything. And I told them it's not even a big deal, really. Christmas is just...it's just not a big deal, you know?"

I really don't know. I'd give anything to be with Quinn right now.

"Mom is probably going to come in the first week of January, though. Once prices on flights go down a little."

We each another slice of pizza in silence before I finally get the nerve to ask her outright.

"Alright, Linney. We've known each other since we were fifteen," I say. I think about how the first time I talked to

Linney was when I was defending her in our class full of assholes, and how that need to protect her has never really completely gone away. That it's what brought me back here today. So I need to know. I need to know what she's up against so that I can help her. Because right now, I'm thinking any number of things, and none of them are good. I'm hoping that my mind is just preparing me for the worst case scenario, that it isn't actually anything bad. I slide my hand across the booth and clutch her dainty fingers. Her touch is familiar in a way that it shouldn't be. I shouldn't remember it this clearly. And after pulling away from her earlier, I shouldn't be instigating anything. So why do I do it? "Here's the part where you tell me what the hell is going on."

"I feel like it's been built up too much now, and you came all this way because you were worried about me and now I just feel stupid."

"Don't," I say. "I came because I wanted to."

"I don't know what I did to deserve a friend like you, but it's really nice to know that you cared enough to fly all the way out here, not even knowing what you're walking into. I meant it earlier when I said you were a good guy, Ben. The best." She squeezes my hand like she's latching on to a life raft. Frantic and needy. And it makes me so damn glad that I came. So glad that it's my hand she's grasping onto.

"Linney, what happened?"

She takes a deep breath, and then lets it out slowly. "Nick, you remember Nick Barker, right?"

I nod. "Sure."

Nick went to the same high school as Linney and I before I moved to Atlanta. I hadn't really been friends with him, but I knew of him.

"I started seeing him not long after the time that I saw you last year, when I was here looking at colleges." It's impossible to hear her talk about the last time that she was here in town and not think of the fall-out with Quinn.

"And things were great for a long time. I started classes over the summer at the University of Kentucky, and he was at the University of Tennessee. It was okay being apart because we were both so busy with school, and he'd come in on weekends so that was good."

Linney looks around the deserted restaurant.

"Two weekends in a row I had plans with the Chi Omega girls and I couldn't get together with Nick. I didn't think it was such a big deal, but he freaked. He showed up at my dorm in the middle of the night, convinced I was with someone else there. He was screaming outside of the building because the girls wouldn't let him in. He kicked the door in,

Ben." Linney's cheeks turn the deepest red I've ever seen on her pale face. "I was humiliated. These girls were new friends, and he made a fool out of me. Of course he apologized, but mama told me I wasn't allowed to see him anymore after that. I didn't care. I was so angry and embarrassed. I didn't *want* to see him."

I can't imagine someone as quiet and polite as Linney being yelled at by some prick. The thought of her holed up in her dorm while he beat the door down doesn't sit well with me. I involuntarily clench my fist with anger.

"Well, staying away from him…that didn't go over well at all. Nick started showing up during the week when he should have been in class in a different state. I mean, who does that? He would just sit in his car and watch us while we painted signs for events, or stare at my dorm. He was calling my phone so many times a day, I ended up getting so frustrated that I threw it in the garbage and bought a new one."

"So, that's why you changed your number?" I ask, remembering the quick, cryptic text that Linney sent me a while back from a new number. I didn't reply to it. What an asshole.

Linney nods. "It was just crazy. Mama and the counselors told me that if I just kept ignoring him, he'd get bored and leave me alone. But he didn't."

I feel a twisting in my gut watching Linney retell the story, the fear present in her eyes even hundreds of miles away from this douche and sitting here with me, where she knows I'd do anything in the world to protect her. I want to beat the shit out of this clown.

"I started finding cards from him under my windshield wipers, gifts outside of my dorm room, it was all just creepy. One day when I came back from class, there were dozens of roses outside my door room door. He must have spent a fortune. I threw them all away. The more he tried to do 'nice' things, the more creeped out I got."

"Did you call the police?" I work my jaw back and forth.

"Yeah, Dad did. They had us fill out a report, but he hadn't really done anything harmful, you know? It was just more annoying than anything."

"Then why'd you come here?"

Linney takes a deep breath. "I came home from a party one night. A bunch of the girls wanted to stay late, but I was tired, so I left alone, which was stupid. I know that, please don't tell me again. My dad never misses an opportunity to tell me how stupid that was, especially with everything that was already going on."

She blots the grease off the top of a piece of pizza with a napkin over and over until it's so dry, it could be repackaged and labeled as health food.

"Linney." I press.

"So, when I get to my dorm, the door is unlocked, which was weird because I was so vigilant about keeping it locked. Just not vigilant enough to get someone to walk me home, I guess. Anyway, as soon as I walked in and closed the door behind me, I saw him sitting there."

Linney clutches her stomach and it makes my own stomach turn.

"He, um..." She scratches at her arms nervously and rocks back and forth in her chair. "Crap, I really don't like talking about this. Even to you. Especially to you."

"Did the bastard rape you, Linney? Please don't tell me that." I ignored her calls. I didn't reply to her texts. Please don't tell me that some asshole put his hands on her.

"No," she says. "No, but he tried. Unlucky for Nick, my roommate, Bethany, didn't know that I had left the party and came back to our room with her boyfriend. Lucky for me, Bethany's boyfriend could bench press Nick."

"Oh, shit, Linney. You should have called me earlier, before it got that far, before he could try to hurt you—before you had to move away. I'm so sorry I wasn't there." It isn't possible for me to feel any worse about myself than I do right now. How could I let her down like this?

"Thank you for saying that. Really. But there wasn't anything that you could do to prevent it, and besides, you have your own girlfriend to worry about," Caroline says. I know she doesn't mean it as a dig, so why does it so closely resemble one?

"I just wish all guys were more like you, Ben. I never would have let you go if I knew what the rest of them were like."

I would have stayed if it meant being able to protect you from that. The thought runs through my mind, but it shouldn't ever exist, no matter what the situation with Linney is.

"What happened to him? Nick, I mean?" I ask.

"He was arrested, which is great, but his dad got him out. Small town politics at its best, right? I'm not sure what's going to happen now, but the second he was released Mom and Dad had me on the first flight out of Kentucky. And, that's it. That's why I'm crashing your family Christmas."

"You aren't. I'm glad you're with them. I'm glad you're safe."

I push my chair out and walk around the table just as Linney does the same. She clings to my side and crushes into me, her small arms wrapping around me. I pull her in and hold her close.

"This feels safe," she says.

And I know that I can't let her go.

Twelve

Quinn

I stare outthe kitchen window, watching the children of this quiet, medieval town run up and down the steep hill, dressed in red tights and green hats and looking every bit like something out of a fairytale. I hope it's real. I hope those kids are as happy as the smiles on their faces portray.

I know it sounds strange to even be bothered by this, because, for the most part, my family is a bunch of dillholes, but I can't help but miss them on Christmas Eve. And I'd be lying if I said I wasn't just a little jealous that Carter gets to hang out with our brother, Mason, today. Mason may be spoiled, but I love him and hope he grows up okay in that house alone. It's even more hurtful that my parents cared so little that I wasn't going to make it home. When I called and told them about this trip, Mom barely gave a reaction at all. I'll give her the benefit of the doubt that it was because she was doped up on whatever holiday concoction she took to deal with Dad, but come on, it's *Italy*. She could have at least pretended to be excited for me, right? Instead, she changed the subject to tell me about how Mason was selected for a new Winter Ball team and was the new pitcher. I'm proud of my brother, but why didn't I ever get to exist?

The laneways of Spello are decorated with garlands and bows and bits of fake snow, but not in a gaudy way like we Americans do it up. I smile every time I walk outside and see the dainty Christmas bulbs hanging from the potted plants outside of each home, and, even though I'm not religious, the Nativity-crib displays always choke me up with their simplistic beauty and the fact that they mean so much to the people here. I want to believe in something like they believe.

I thought for sure my day would get better by talking to Ben, but I haven't been able to get him on the phone in days. Maybe he's at home sulking that he's alone. Maybe he's out taking pictures of the dudes on the surfboards wearing Santa hats. Or maybe he's avoiding me because he's angry that I came here after all. I don't think that's it. But it could be. My paranoia kicks into high gear after the sixth ring.

I listen to the familiar robotic voice tell me to leave a message after the tone and hang up, slamming my phone onto the table top.

"I don't understand why he won't just answer the phone!" I yell. "He's seriously making me crazy."

Amalea looks up from the bag that she's carefully packing snacks and wine in and smiles that knowing smile that tells me she's about to dole out one of her chips of wisdom.

"If you've never gone mad, you've never really been in love," she says.

"Helpful." I smirk. "What are you doing anyway? Can I help?"

"It's Christmas Eve. We're going to *Città di Castello* to see the boats."

"Boats?"

"The boats on the Tiber River." She frequently does this. She says things in a way like I should obviously understand them or know exactly what she's talking about, when in reality, I only do about two-percent of the time. She sighs."The canoeists decorate their boats with lights, and dress as Father Christmas and float down the river. Put on something warmer, too. You're going to freeze, silly girl."

"Yes, ma'am," I say. I can't fight the smile. I want to stay here and mope that Ben won't answer my calls for whatever reason and that Carter is home with Mason and my parents, but I'm in Italy and I am going to embrace it and go enjoy the hell out of these canoes.

I race upstairs to grab my coat. When I come back down, Chef Davide is standing in the doorway. I back up, quietly, hoping that he and Amalea don't hear me, but it's too late. I have the worst luck.

"Quinn, *Buon Natale!*" Davide calls from the door. Amalea turns and sees me, and then politely backs up to let Davide in.

"Merry Christmas," I reply.

I've never seen him wearing anything but his chef's coat, but tonight, Davide is dressed in dark gray pants and a wool blazer and looks pretty damn dapper. For a teacher.

"I don't mean to interrupt your evening. I didn't know if you two had plans, and I'm going to *Città di Castello.* Would you both be interested in joining me?"

"We were headed there ourselves," Amalea says. She taps her hand absently on the doorframe. Her nervousness is adorable.

"Perfetto!" Chef says.

"Actually," I say, backing up two steps. "I was just coming down to tell you that I didn't feel up to going anywhere tonight."

Amalea narrows her eyes at me and purses her lips, silently scolding me for my obvious lie.

"That gelato I ate earlier...You told me it wasn't a good idea in this weather, but I don't ever listen, right?" I laugh.

In reality, the salted caramel gelato was delicious and I don't regret a solitary bite of it.

"I know you were so looking forward to it and I hate that I'll miss it, but I really ought to lie down for a while. I think you should go, though," I say. "*With* Davide."

A blush ignites under Amalea's olive cheeks. "Chef Baldassare does not want to spend his evening with just me."

"I doubt he minds," I say, pushing Amalea and the vein in her forehead, to near stroke level.

"I would love to accompany you," Davide says.

"See there," I smirk outwardly, but inside, I'm honestly not looking forward to spending the holiday alone. And even though the idea of missing out on an Italian tradition, when this may be my only Christmas that I ever spend here, has me feeling pretty freaking low, I guess the reality is that it's only fair, since Ben is missing out on a festive Christmas, too. I just hope he's not eating Ramen. Please don't let him be eating Ramen. "You guys go! Enjoy! And please take pictures, I want to show Ben when I get home!"

Amalea's eyes trail across the room to Davide and then back to me, weighing her options. Or plotting to kill me. She must decide I'm too much trouble to dispose of, because she grabs her coat off of the hook and steps out into the night air. I'm about to head back up the small staircase when Davide turns to me.

"*Grazie,*" he says with a polite nod. And I know that at least one of our Christmas wishes has come true. For me and Ben, Christmas last year was a fresh start, and I really hope that somehow, Amalea and Davide can have their own slates wiped clean tonight.

I lie back on my bed and dial Ben's cell phone again.

"Just answer the phone," I say. It comes out sounding more like a beg than a request.

Just kiss me. I remember silently pleading last Christmas.

"Hi, it's me again," I say to Ben's voicemail. "I know, I know, I'm pretty much stalking you at this point. But, I wanted to catch you to say Merry Christmas. I don't know what your plans are, but I'm just sort of hanging out, so call me back. It doesn't matter what time it is. I just really want to talk to you. I miss your voice. I miss you." *'I love you, too,' I whispered in his ear, saying the words to him for the first time that night that we made love for the first time.* "I love you, Ben."

I hang up the phone and I'm not sure what to do. I could eat— *again*. I could drink a bottle of the Lambrusco that Amalea introduced me to, but drinking alone on Christmas Eve just sounds sad. Instead, I call Carter, who unlike my boyfriend, answers on the first ring.

"Merry Christmas, Quinnlette!" Carter says. I can't help but smile, hearing a familiar voice.

"Back atcha. How are you? How's Mason?" I ask. Part of the reason I stayed at home for so long was because the idea of leaving Mason behind with my parents and their drama had guilt eating at me daily. At least if I was there, they could take their craziness out on me. But leaving Mason alone… He's different than Carter and me. More sensitive. More sheltered. I know he's seen more than he's let on, but I also know that I liked being the one to help shield him from some of the insanity. The fights. The broken dishes. Mom MIA for weeks at a time. As far as Mason knew, Mom went on solo mini-vacay's. He didn't know she was gone for things like extended hospital stays for threatening to harm herself, near overdoses, and stints in rehab. What about now? Now that Carter and I are both gone? It keeps me up some nights. I feel selfish for choosing a life with Ben far away from the madness. But before I left, things had gotten bad. Really, really bad. What choice did I have but to leave?

"Mason's good. From the looks of the pile of loot under the tree, he's about to make out like a damn sheik," he says as he laughs. "He's bummed you're not here, though."

"I wish I was. I wish all of us were together."

"Maybe next year. I'll tell you what, I miss your baking and cooking for sure right now."

I smile, feeling proud of myself that I at least have something good to offer.

"You're having a good time, though?" Carter asks.

"I'm having a great time. I'm just maybe ready to come home," I say. I flip onto my side and wish I could teleport myself back to my apartment. Even though I know I'm going to miss Italy something fierce, I think it's time to go home. "I miss you guys. I miss Ben—hell, I miss just *talking* to Ben. I miss a bed that is big enough for me to stretch out in, and—"

Carter's voice dips a little lower. "Wait, you haven't talked to Ben?"

"A couple of times. I guess he's busy. Probably spending a lot of time in the darkroom since Ron is out of town until after the New Year, you know? He has this thing about never bringing his phone in with him when he's working." A chill runs through me, thinking of the last time I was in the darkroom with Ben.

"Right," Carter says, cautiously. "I'm sure that's all it is."

His cautious voice scrapes at me because Carter loves Ben. I know it's my paranoia ringing in again, and I won't let it ruin whatever kind of holiday loneliness I've dug myself into.

"Anyway, how's Shayna doing? Her family is glad to have her home, right?"

"Yeah, they sort of hold a monopoly over her. I haven't seen her since yesterday. I'm going to go and have dinner at her folks' house later, but it's weird not having her around, you know? Guess I've kind of gotten used to having her with me all the time. It's…nice."

"I know," I say. I can empathize with Carter better than anyone right now.

"Of course you do. Hey, Mom is just about done making breakfast, you want to talk to her?"

"Our mom is actually cooking?" Wow, maybe things do change.

"I didn't say it was a good thing, I just said there was about to be food. That we can try to eat," he says with a laugh.

"Actually, I'm pretty beat. I think I'll just give her a call tomorrow, if that's okay?"

"Sure thing, Quinnlette. Hey, have a safe trip home."

"I will, thanks. You guys, too. I've got the perfect idea for a souvenir for Shayna, and it's not jewelry so don't get her hopes up."

"Do you need Shay and me to pick you up from the airport?"

I slide the nail of my index finger under the Christmas-red polish on my thumb and slice it off in a single layer. "No, Ben should be there. He has my flight info."

"Okay…" Carter pauses. "If you're sure. But give me a call if something comes up."

"Thanks, bro. Tell everyone that I said Merry Christmas," I say.

When I hang up, I suddenly know just what to do with my evening.

I pad lightly down the stairs, and back into the small kitchen.

I rummage through Amalea's cabinets, digging for plain ingredients to make something simple and comforting. I pull out flour, sugar, butter and other basicsand arrange them neatly on the counter top, and then get to work. I work at a frantic pace at first, creaming the butter and adding the dry ingredients in a frenzy. But once I pluck an orange from the fruit bowl on the table and zest it into the bowl, the fresh, citrusy aroma invades my nostrils and calms me like a baby being rocked to sleep with a familiar lullaby.

Once the dough is rolled out, I pinch off small pieces and tie them into loose knots before baking them. While the sugar cookies bake, I make a bowl of icing and find some colorful sprinkles buried deep in the cabinet.

When the cookies are baked, iced, and covered in a generous dousing of sugared confetti, I sit back to enjoy a small glass of Lambrusco and bite into one of masterpieces. They aren't anything fancy, but they are exactly what I needed. They remind me of baking at home while Mason watched, perched on top of a barstool with his knobby knees tucked under him. I lethim decorate the cookies, even though the control freak in me physically hurt watching him pipe uneven coats of icing on the tops and not decorating them the way I'd envisioned.

I find a small cardboard box in the pantry and fill it with the remaining cookies, and tie a piece of red yarn around it. Amalea will be able to enjoy the rest of the cookies with her cappuccino on Christmas morning.

It may not be much, but it's a small token of how thankful I am for Amalea welcoming me into her home, for teaching me how to make amazing dishes, and opening up her past to me as well. I know first-hand how hard it is to admit you've fucked up. I know how hard it is to let people in. She was willing to let me, of all people, in. And that feels incredible.

I'm grateful for my time here in Italy. And right now, *grateful* is the best place to be.

Thirteen

BEN

I wake up Christmas morning with Linney's head on my shoulder, her blond hair fuzzy and tickling my nose. We'd fallen asleep on the sofa in the basement together after a long night with a marathon of holiday movies, and store-bought cookies—that were a little disappointing after getting so used to Quinn's baking. But on the upside, I got Caroline to drink some spiked eggnog with me.

Caroline and I haven't talked much about what had gone on with Nick since we left Fellini's that afternoon. I want her to know that she's safe here, and that she can leave all of that behind. I just don't know how I can be there for her like I want to. My life is back in California. My job, school, my apartment. And Quinn will be back in a matter of days. I need to call Quinn, but once I talk to her, I don't know how to hide where I am. And I really don't want to tell her while she's still across the world. Not only because I don't want to ruin her trip like Carter warned me about. I don't want her to hurt when I'm not there to explain. I know if I could just explain things, what happened with Caroline and Nick, so that even if she's angry, she'd understand. She has to.

I slip a pillow under her head at the same time that I pull my arm out from under her and walk quietly up the stairs and into the living room. My mom is sitting by the tree, coffee cup in hand, like she's done every Christmas morning since I was a kid. She'll sit there, waiting for me to open presents, so she can watch my reactions—and where I put the wrapping paper when I'm done.

"Morning," I say, rubbing my hair into an even bigger mess than it probably already was.

"Good morning, Ben. Were you down there with Caroline?"

I know she already knows the answer to this, and I know her rules.

"Yeah, Ma, we fell asleep. No big deal."

She pulls her lips into a tight line, but doesn't argue. Because it's Caroline. Because my relationship with my mom would be worlds different if I were in love with Caroline instead of Quinn.

I stare at the neatly stacked presents under the tree, hoping she didn't get me anything. After lunch with Caroline the other day, we skipped shopping altogether and I didn't get my parents a thing. *Dick.*

Mom plucks a perfectly wrapped package from the stack and hands it to me.

"I didn't know what to get you, we never talk anymore." She can't resist getting a dig in. "You can return it if you like."

"Thanks," I say. "You didn't have to do that."

"I'm your mother, of course I did."

I stand there awkwardly holding the gift until she nudges my hands.

"Oh, open it, Benny. That's what gifts are made for," Mom says.

I obediently slide the twine off of the box and carefully peel back the layer of green wrapping paper, knowing that she's watching me, scrutinizing how I unwrap the gift.

Inside is what at first, looks like a wallet, but after I pull it out, I realize that it's foldable solar panels.

"You can charge your camera batteries on that, if you're ever in a jam," Mom says. She tightens her robe and looks down at her coffee cup. This is the first time she's ever acknowledged what I love to do without ridiculing it in some way. For years she's told me what a useless hobby photography is. How my time would be better suited pursuing a worthwhile career. But this catches me off guard in the best way. Because it's a door opening. One that will allow me to do what I love and not have to hide it. And maybe, it's leaving a little room to allow *who* I love into the picture, too.

"This is incredible. Thank you."

I pull her in for a quick hug. I may be grown, but hugging my mom on Christmas still feels pretty damn good.

"I'm sorry I don't have a gift for you. I didn't expect to be here, and…we haven't talked much…" I feel like a world-class asshole right now, being here on Christmas morning and not having a single thing for my parents.

"The homemade biscotti that Quinn sent was enough," Mom says, folding a blanket with military precision and tucking it away in the trunk that houses blankets only, no exceptions.

My mind is reeling. Quinn sent my parents a gift? Why didn't she tell me?

"The look on your face tells me you didn't know about that?" Mom says. "It was delicious, came right after Thanksgiving."

"I didn't know, no."

"Your father said I should check it for nails or arsenic."

"Ma—"

"Oh, lighten up, Benny, it was a joke. It was a lovely gesture. Please thank her for us."

"Yeah, I will. I'm glad that she did that."

"It shows a lot of maturity that she did without even telling you, you know. It surprises me."

"I think if you got to know her, Ma, a lot about Quinn would surprise you."

"I don't know if I'm ready for that, Ben. But I'm glad that you're here, now. Even if part of me still wishes you were here because you were proposing to that lovely girl in there." Mom motions into the den where Caroline has snuck upstairs without me noticing and is doing a puzzle with my dad. It should make me feel good, knowing that she is so comfortable here with my family, but instead, it just makes me angry because Quinn has never had that chance with them.

"You know, Ma," I say. "Part of the reason I loved being with Quinn in the first place is because she was the exact opposite of all of this." Because with Quinn, there were no limits. There weren't these strict, rigid rules. Because Quinn was everything that my mom couldn't stand. And even if I didn't mean to, I fell completely in love with her.

"I know that. Of course I know that," my mom says. "You don't think I know that my micromanaging of your life drove you away? And right to that girl? Of course it did. She has problems, Benny. You should have run the opposite direction. But no, it made you want to take care of people just as much as I do, just in a totally different way. My way is strict and no-nonsense. But you, Ben, you've wanted to take care of people in the way that your heart told you to. I haven't always agreed with the choices that you've made—"

"That's an understatement, Ma. You made me choose." And I'd make the same choice again. Every single time. I love the life Quinn and I have, and my stupid ass insecurities about what she's doing and experiencing without me will never compare to how fiercely I love that woman.

And standing here, talking to my mom, seeing Caroline settled into their perfect existence, I know that I've done all I can here. I came to be a friend to Caroline, and I'm glad that I was, but I need to get back to my life with Quinn.

"I was wrong to do that. Especially because I knew that if I gave you a choice that I'd end up the loser."

"Ma—" I say. I'm glad she cuts me off. I don't know how to respond to that. It's the truth, but it feels like shit to admit it.

"It's okay. It's the truth. I knew you wouldn't walk away from that girl—"

"Quinn, her name is *Quinn*." I can't wrap my mind around the disrespect that Mom continues to show someone she knows means the fucking world to me.

"I know it is. Just like I *knew* you'd never walk away from *Quinn*."

"Then why'd you do it? Why'd you give me that dumb ultimatum if you didn't think I'd do what you wanted?"

"I was just so scared that you were ruining your chance for a good future, Benny. But what was I supposed to do? I couldn't condone it, Ben. I *couldn't*. My entire adult life has been spent taking care of you. You don't even realize that my whole identity is wrapped up in how well I took care of you. If you failed, I failed, Benny."

"I'm not failing, Ma. I'm doing really well," I say. "School's going great. I just sold some of my work, and I'm happy Mom, I really am. I wish you could see that."

"I'm glad that things are working out for you now, Ben. And no, I haven't always agreed with your choices. I wish you would have made different ones. I know you don't want to hear that, but it's the truth. I wish you would have chosen someone else. Someone who does the right thing. Someone who gets along with your family. Someone who challenges you—"

I can't help but laugh, because one thing that Quinn does every single day is challenge me.

"Don't laugh, Ben. The choices you've made wouldn't have been the ones that I would have made for you, but I am proud of you. *I am.*" And her words may not seem like much to anyone else, but to me, I know that my mom is opening her perfectly crafted world just a little to the idea that Quinn is here to stay. At least I hope she is.

And in that moment, my mind flashes to Carter seeing Caroline and I together, and I just hope to God I get the chance to explain it all to her before he says anything.

"Thanks, Ma."

"I've got to go get dressed. Brunch in an hour," she says. She hugs me again. "One hour, Benny."

I wait until Mom has left the room and pull my phone out of my pocket. I don't take the time to calculate what time it is in Quinn's end of the world before it's already ringing.

And this time, I'm the one talking to a voicemail box.

"Hey, doll. I don't know what time it is there, but it's Christmas morning here and I miss you so damn much today. I hope you're having an amazing time, and I can't wait to see you. Love you, baby." She's just busy. Or sleeping. But I have to believe Carter didn't tell her.

Fourteen

QUINN

"Are you all packed?" Amalea asks.

"I think so," I say. I mailed several boxes of wine, balsamic vinegar, and books back to the States earlier in the week, so I'm down to just my one, red suitcase. Same as when I started, but I'm so completely different.

"Are you ready?"

I trace the stitching on the quilt that I've been sleeping under for the last month. I don't think I'll ever be ready to leave this place— or ready to leave Amalea.

"I guess, but the train doesn't leave for another three hours," I say.

"*Sciocchezza!*" Amalea says. She throws her hands up. "No train for you. I will take you to Rome."

"No way. That's over a two hour drive," I say, shaking my head. "You don't have to do that. The train is fine."

"I know that I don't *have* to, Quinn. I want to." I can't believe they're the same words Ben said to me at the airport.

"Okay. I'd love that, thank you." I smile. "Is Davide coming along for the ride, too?" I slip in his name, because

Amalea hasn't mentioned him since they spent Christmas Eve together.

Amalea cuts her eyes at me. "You stupid girl." She laughs. It's not my favorite nickname, but at least I know it's meant to be endearing.

We load my luggage into her small Fiat, make a stop at the *Pasticcceria* at the bottom of the hill so that I can buy Shayna these darling cookies that look like real peaches that I saw my first day in town and make our way to Rome.

The drive is beautiful, full of rolling hills and dotted with ancient ruins. I wish I would have gotten out to see more while I was here, but there will be a next time. This time was for cooking and learning, and finding out just how much I can do on my own. I've already promised Amalea that I'll be back, with Ben.

I decide to call Ben once more before we get to the airport. I should be furious that I haven't been able to talk to him as much as I want, but with the crappy signal in Spello, and the time change, I guess it's forgivable. But he's going to owe me when I get back home. And the thought of being back in his arms, in our bed, is enough to smooth the frayed nerves.

"Baby?" My heart goes tachycardic at the sound of his voice. It isn't until I'd hear it again that I realize just how much I've missed it.

"Ben, oh, god I'm so glad to hear your voice. I'm on my way to the airport right now and I love you so much and I can't wait to see you!" I cram it all into one excited breath.

"You—no—miss—too." His voice cuts in and out and I could cry out of frustration.

"I can't hear you. I'm in the car on the way to the airport. Damn hills!"

"I'll—you—soon—love."

"Fuck," I say. Amalea gives me a disapproving glance, and I hang up the phone, feeling defeated.

"I finally get him on the phone and the service is complete and total shit again! Sorry, crap."

"You'll see him soon."

"How about you? When will you see your man again?" I'm pressing my luck, I know. Amalea may leave me in the Italian countryside without a map if I keep it up.

"Things are not so simple for Davide and I as they are for you and your Ben."

I laugh. "Things are never simple with Ben. I just love him too much to walk away, I guess."

Amalea shrugs. "I think Davide and I are more complicated still."

"Are you saying you can't work things out with Davide?" Amalea considers her words for a minute. "I'm staying I don't know yet. Sometimes life hands you jagged pieces to the puzzle, Quinn. They won't fit together no matter how hard you try."

"But you love him," I say matter-of-factly, feeling like the romantic sap I'm definitely not.

Amalea shrugs her delicate shoulders. "In a perfect, neat world, love should be all that matters. But sometimes, it's not. Sometimes it's hard too hard to hold all of the pieces together."

The Quinn of last year would agree with her. That love is too complicated. That hearts are worth protecting at any cost. But right now, on my way home to see Ben, I don't believe any of those things, and I have to bite my tongue. I want Amalea to be happy, and I hope that Davide will fight for her like I think he will. It may just take time.

The ride takes longer than we had anticipated, and I'm left with a quick, curbside good-bye. It's probably better that way. I've always been terrible with good-byes.

"I think you should try. With Davide, I mean," I say.

I lean in to kiss Amalea's cheeks, but she pulls me in for a tight embrace instead.

"I love you, stupid girl," she says. And I cry harder than I have during any good-bye I can remember.

I want to tell Amalea all of the things that this trip has meant to me. The words climb up my throat, trying to string themselves into the perfect arrangement, before dissolving and slinking back down. Unspoken.

I learned to how to cook wild boar sauce in Italy. I learned how to make pasta and a perfectly crusty ciabbata. But from Amalea, I learned far more important lessons. I learned sfogliatelle is quite possibly the most labor intensive food I've ever prepared—but like most things, worth the effort. I learned that Grappa never goes down smooth, no matter what you eat with it. And I learned that letting go of guilt can open the door to happiness and second chances

"I love you. More," I say.

Fifteen

BEN

I hang up with Quinn, grinning like a jackass. I have no clue whether or not she could hear a word that I was saying, but hearing her voice again, knowing that she's on her way home—nothing else matters.

"That was Quinn?" Caroline asks, standing in the doorway to my old room. I straighten my smile a bit so I look a little less like a fool.

"Yep," I say. I carefully pack my camera in my bag and set it on the edge of my bed along with my duffel. "Listen, Linney, I'm heading home today, but I don't want you to think that that means that I'm not here for you."

Her shoulders curl in and she gives a disappointed frown.

"Mom said that your parents are working on a restraining order and that you may be able to go home soon, and I'm always a call away, you know that right?"

"Will Quinn let you call me?" she asks.

It's a valid question, I guess, but the acid-laced tone Caroline wraps it up in catches me off guard.

"I'm sure she'll understand. Once I have a chance to explain it to her."

"And if she doesn't? Then what am I supposed to do?"

I let the question rewind and repeat in my head a few times, trying to come up with a suitable answer.

"Linney, it's going to be okay. Trust me." I pull her in for a quick hug and feel her body go slack in my arms. She's relaxed, and I'm reminded of what she said the other day in the restaurant. *This feels safe.* I pull her in tighter and rest my chin on top of her head. I don't know what more I can do for her, but right now, this appears to be enough.

"Benny, you forgot to pack th—" Mom interrupts, holding my Kindle.

Caroline pulls away and walks out of the room, not taking her eyes off of the floor.

"Thanks, Ma," I say, stashing the e-reader into my carry-on. "It was good to see you and Pop."

"You too. I'm glad you came. I really didn't know what I was going to do, my first Christmas without my boy around." As soon as the words leave her mouth, she realizes that it's not true. Because last year, I missed Christmas with her. Last year, I was with *my* girl.

"Maybe next year we can all be together," I say.

Mom doesn't reply, but she doesn't spit in my face either, so I'll call it progress.

"Listen, I'm going to take a shower before I leave for the airport." I can't wait to be back in California. I should beat Quinn in by several hours, enough time to make it home and change and make sure the apartment is clean. I don't remember how it looked when I left, I ran out in such a hurry to get to Atlanta. It seems like months, not days, since I was in our home, eating crappy food, alone. I was so miserable that last day in town, but now I can't wait to get back.

"Don't forget to say good-bye to your dad and me. And re-pack that bag, it looks terrible," Mom says. I laugh as I glance down at my duffel, crammed full of unfolded clothes. I was hardly able to zip the damn thing.

"Sure thing, Ma." I kiss her cheek before she walks away.

I gather up a fresh change of clothes, turn the shower to scalding hot and step inside. I tip my head back into the heavy stream of water and let my mind wander to how much I'm looking forward to having my shower mate back when Quinn and I are home again.

"Ben?" Caroline's voice interrupts my thoughts at the worst possible time.

I clear my throat. "Yeah," I rasp out.

Do I peer out from behind the curtain? Do I turn off the water?

"I know it's weird that I'm in here, we haven't— I mean, it's probably not appropriate. You're just leaving and this just couldn't wait."

Linney and I never had sex when we were together—or ever. It's not like I'm a total prude, we did other things. We've seen each other naked. But she's right, her being in here is not the best idea.

"What's up, Linney? I'll be out in just a second."

"I just want you to know that you have options. I mean, I know you say you're happy there in California, but we were happy once, too."

"Linney—"

"Just let me finish. I know your mom doesn't like Quinn like she loves me. And it'd make your life so much easier if you had someone in it that got along with her, right?"

She's right. My life would be easier. But would it be better?

"And we've known each other forever. We always got along. The only reason we broke up in the first place is because you moved here. But I can move here. Or wherever you are. I don't care. Because you're good for me…and you're safe…and I miss you." Her voice changes. Desperation clings to each word.

"I can't just stay here, Linney. I have a life there. I have school. And a job. And an apartment and Quinn. I have *Quinn* there."

"But I need you, Ben. God I need you. The last few days are the safest I've felt in months."

I feel like the asshole of the century talking to her through a shower curtain, but I don't know what else to do. I want to be there for Caroline, but I can't be her savior. *I can't.* What the fuck did I do? I brought every bit of this on myself. I thought that coming here would help Caroline, but it's made things into an even bigger mess, one that I can't save her from.

Quinn was right. Of course she was. Linney wants more, maybe she always will.

"You could just stay," she says. Her voice is small and wounded and I want to pull the shower curtain back and tell her it's going to be okay and that things will calm down and work out for her. That I'm sorry that I can't be the one to do it for her. But the reality is, I'm standing her wet and naked and my doing that would straighten any blurry line that I've been straddling by being in Atlanta in the first place.

"I love you, Ben. I never did stop loving you. You know that, I told you last year. And once upon a time, you loved me, too," she says.

I did love her once.And the feeling to protect her and be there for her didn't just disappear, even if it's wrong.

The curtain moves and Linney is there. And it's wrong in so many different ways. She ignores the stream of water, soaking her clothes and making them stick to her skin in a way that I shouldn't even be noticing. She stands on her tip toes and catches my earlobe between her teeth— something she knows I've never been able to resist.

"Just stay," she whispers.

Sixteen

QUINN

I feel like I've been sitting here for hours, but it's probably been more like twenty minutes. I slide my iPhone out of my pocket and check the time, and to see if Ben has called. *Again.* He hasn't.

LA has a shit ton of traffic, I get it. But I haven't seen him in a month, we've barely talked on the phone, and I sort of just had this idea that there would be this cinematic reunion once I got passed the baggage claim.

But instead, it's just me.

Sitting curbside outside of the airport, waiting for his familiar car to pull up.

But it doesn't.

~~~~~~~~~~~~~~~~

"Thanks for coming to get me," I say to Carter as he tosses my suitcase into the back of his Jeep.

"No sweat, Quinnlette. How was it?" He's beaming back at me and I am so happy that someone is here and glad to see me.

"Amazing. Obviously. Where's Ben?"

Carter glances over his shoulder before he pulls out into traffic and ignores my question.

"Carter?" I press. Heat simmers under my skin. What is going on? I search my memory for what I might have said wrong--*done* wrong--to make him not be here to pick me up after four weeks away.

"What, your brother isn't good enough? I see how it is," Carter jokes.

Carter rubs his palm on the back of his neck and looks everywhere but at me.

"What the hell is going on?"

"Fuck Ben for putting me in the situation that I have to be the one to tell you this, because I like the asshole, but you're my sister—"

"Carter. Tell me." I feel tears prickle in the corners of my eyes. He hasn't even answered my question yet, but all sorts of things are flying through my mind that all involved Ben realizing what a loser I am, and packing his bags.

"He went to spend the holidays with his parents," Carter finally says. He blows out a deep breath, but doesn't look relieved to have that out of the way.

"Oh," I say. I jerk my head back in surprise that that's all he was worried about telling me. I'm surprised Ben didn't tell me, but I'm glad he went home to see his family after all.

"But, I thought he didn't end up going with you?"

"He didn't. Shay and I left on our own. We ran into him though, in Atlanta." He says it in a leading way, like he's baiting me to ask more, and it makes my stomach churn.

"Cool, did you guys hang out? Did he come to the house?" I know that's not what Carter is getting at. I know it. But I still hope it's something as simple as that.

He shakes his head and turns down our street.

"Shay and I went down to Little Five Points to grab a slice of White Pizza," he pauses to glance over at me, "I know it's not pizza in Napoli, but it was damn good, you know."

"I get it, pizza…back to Ben."

"So, we were sort of surprised to see him there."

"With his parents?"

Carter gives a sharp, quick shake of his head.

"Who?"

"I didn't recognize her, but Shay said she looked familiar. He seemed really…awkward. Maybe worried that we saw him? I don't know how to explain it. He definitely wasn't himself, though. He introduced her to us, and she was nice enough."

"Who?" I press. My hands are shaking. A surge of heat under my skin rages through me. *What the hell is Ben doing?*

"Caroline," Carter says. He says it with regret, like he pities me and that makes my guttural rage and sadness take over every fiber of me. "He said he'd to be back last night, but I never saw him. When you called, I stopped by your apartment to see if he'd just overslept, but he wasn't there, either."

"I understand," I say.

"I tried calling him, but it went straight to voicemail."

"Yeah, me too," I say. My voice is becoming softer, weaker, it feels like the air has been sucked out of my lungs, leaving me struggling to breath and the world spinning out of control.

Because of her.

"So, you knew all of that, when I called you on Christmas? Why didn't you tell me then?"

Carter shakes his head and sighs, "Quinn, that would have ruined the last few days of your trip, no way was I doing that with you that far away."

The last few words make me pause. He was worried I'd do something stupid. Like the last time things were rough with Ben and I ended up in the hospital. But that was completely different and had little to do with Ben and more to do with the fact that I was seriously out of my mind for a while. I've done so much better since then. I went to therapy for months, I took the meds they gave me. I've changed. *Right?*

"What was the point in telling you anyway? It could be nothing, Quinnlette. I mean, maybe they just ran into each other, I don't know."

I nod, swallowing hard, trying to drown the lump in my throat.

"Maybe he—"

"Carter, just stop." My voice is barely above a whisper. "Please." The last word squeaks out like air coming out of a balloon. Pathetic.

Carter obediently clamps his mouth shut. I've spent my life worrying about losing people because of my own stupidity, it just never occurred to me before now that I could actually lose someone I love because of something completely out of my hands.

"I'm sorry for snapping," I say. "I'm just worried…He should be home by now, right? So where is he?"

Carter shrugs his shoulders. "Maybe bad weather or something out that way. I'm sure he'll be back soon."

And then what?

"Thanks again, for coming to get me."

"Don't mention it. You'd do it for me."

And it's true. I had rushed off to pick Carter up from the airport before. That summer I met Ben, when everything had just begun. When everything was new and scary, but it was a different the fear I have right now.

Ben didn't even try to kiss me good-bye. What the hell? Does he want to keep this platonic or something? Because I sort of had the feeling that you could cut the chemistry with a knife. Did my hair look ridiculous? Was the braid too cutesy to warrant a kiss?

"Gripes!" I yell. I slammed my hand hard onto the steering wheel as I came close to sailing right past my exit while pondering the reason behind Ben's chastity.

I pulled into the airport drop-off lane and reached across to fling the passenger door open before even coming to a complete stop, knowing the security guard was eyeing me with a warning glare.

"Late much?" Carter said. He threw his duffle bag into the cluttered backseat and tossed several empty Mountain Dew bottles off of the passenger seat.

"Sue me."

"Held up at school?"

"Something like that," I mused.

"Jesus, I've been here for thirty minutes and this humidity is already killing me." Carter cranked the air up to the sub-arctic setting.

"Get used to it. It's good to see you, bro," I said.

"You too, Quinnlette." He ruffled my hair the way you would expect a grandparent to.

"Don't do that! You just pulled the braid out of my bangs. And don't call me that, either. I'm not nine."

"Oh chill, you're still my little sister, I'll call you what I want."

Carter and I fought, but I adored him to pieces.

"You didn't forget me, did you?" Carter asked, flicking my arm.

"Never." Yes.

"How's mom?" Carter didn't let his eyes drift from his lap when he asked.

"Same." I shrugged. I wanted to tell him about the nights that Dad had beensneaking out of the house after Mom had passed out. How some nights, he crept back in, clothes all disheveled as if he has just woken up somewhere else. And some nights, he didn't even come home at all. But I couldn't. Carter would have confronted him, and that would have just made things even worse at home. At that time, I didn't even know if I was right or not. It was better to just keep it to myself.

"So, what's up with you and that girl, what's her name? Casey?" I strained my brain to remember the blond from his Facebook picture. "What else is going on? Tell me everything."

"Capri? Nothing's up, we had fun while it lasted. But, ah, Quinnlette, I'm amazing. California is rad. It is so good to be back there. How about you, what's new? What'd you learn at school today?" Carter joked.

I smiled a small, secret grin.

That day, I learned that the boys you haven't yet kissed can be even more special than the ones you have.

"We're home, Quinnlette," Carter shakes my shoulder gently. "Jet lag?"

I peel my face off of the passenger side window. It's stuck nicely while I slept and wipe the sleep from my eyes.

"Sorry, I didn't mean to doze off."

Maybe it was a dream. Maybe Ben is sitting right inside our apartment, tinkering with those damned antique cameras he keeps on the top of the bookshelf that I'll never be able to reach. It drives me crazy that he does that, keeping things just out of my reach. Maybe that's what he was all along. If that's the case, why the fuck did I let myself fall in love with him? I suddenly long to be the same damaged Quinn I was a year ago, so I could just lock myself up in my room and medicate the pain away.

"I'm right down the hall if you need anything else, Quinnlette. I know Shayna's pumped you're home, so come over anytime," Carter says after helping me lug my suitcase into my deserted apartment.

"Thanks," I say. I'm glad that he doesn't try to hug me when he leaves. I feel like if he did, it would make me crumble rather than hold me together.

When Carter leaves, I stand at the doorway staring at the apartment. It looks exactly the same as when I left a month ago. But everything feels different.

I sort of thought that things would stay just like they were before I left. I guess it was naïve, and even selfish, but I really thought things would continue existing like I'd never left. But standing here in my own space, surrounded by my own things, things that Ben and I share, I know that everything has changed. I'll never be able to go back to my exact self before I left for Italy. I'll never see things so one-sided. Cut and dry. Black or white. Things are complex. People are complex. And Ben being with Caroline, well, that changes everything, too.

I start to unpack, but decide to make some tea (tea, since I know that no cup of coffee that I make will compare to the *Caffè alla Nocciola* that Amalea made me the first day I arrived in Italy), grab a blanket off of our bed and curl up on the sofa, tucking my legs under me tightly. But no matter how much I reposition myself, I can't fight off the sick feeling tumbling inside of me. I have no interest in TV or the stack of magazines on the coffee table. I just want to know where Ben is and that he's okay. Because aside from the fact that he was with Caroline, where is he now? He hasn't answered our calls. Does he plan on coming home at all?

~~~~~~~~~~~~~~~~

I don't know what time it is when I feel his lips on my forehead. I fell asleep at some point after calling him an insane amount of times, nearing the triple digits for sure. I don't have to open my eyes to be certain that it's him. There are things that you can never forget, and even though it's been a month, the feeling of Ben's lips on me is one feeling forever engrained in my mind.

For a split second, I sink further into that perfect place between asleep and awake and savor the familiar touch, content to be home and know that Ben's here and safe. Knowing that once I open my eyes, the things that might-be will turn into things that are, and I'm not ready to deal with any of them.

Painful reality sets in too quickly though, and the questions all return.

My eyes gape open.

My fear and anger and insecurity are all present and accounted for, but I can't help but stop and take him in. God, I've missed him.

"Where—"

Ben pulls me in so tightly, it cuts off the words. His lips are on mine, his tongue tracing the inside of my mouth before I can push him away, or even want to. His hand slips up the back of my shirt, to the spot on the small of my back that he loves so much, and presses me in even closer. The warmth and familiarity of him—his touch alone is enough to bring me to my knees. This is how our reunion should have gone. Instead, I was left at the airport. Alone.

I push on his chest to shove him away, shattering the moment— maybe our last one.

"Where were you? I waited," I say.

Ben tightens his jaw and closes his eyes.

"I'm so sorry, I tried to get back here, I just, I was late to the airport and had to get the next flight, and the layover in Denver, Jesus Christ, I thought it'd never end—"

"I sat on the curb and waited, Ben. Carter had to come and pick me up."

The mention of Carter's name is like an ugly cloud floating above Ben and me. He and I just stand there, waiting for the rain to start and drown us.

Ben reaches for my arm, but I jerk it away. It feels foreign to pull away from him. Like my body doesn't want to do it, but it has no choice. Like pulling away from a flame, because you know you'll be burnt.

"I know you know," he says, shifting his weight. "I can explain."

"I don't know if you can," I say. "Did you go there to see her?"

I cross my arms across my chest, creating a barrier between Ben and I, trying to protect my heart. I don't know how we got here.

"Yes."

The simple answer drops off of his lips and suddenly, everything in our world is anything but simple.

"Why, Ben? What are you doing?" I am trying, I really am trying to wrap my mind around what possible explanation he can have that will make this all clear. But I can't think of any scenario that I'm okay with.

"It's not what you're thinking. I went because she was in a bad place, she needed someone."

"In Atlanta? That doesn't even make any sense." I shake my head. Does he think I'm an idiot?

"She's sort of living with my parents," he says.

Time stops. Reverses. *It's two years earlier, and I'm driving to that asshole Mark's house after my run-in with my dad's barely-legal teenage mistress. I'm furious and hurt and I just want Ben to be there for me. But instead, he calls with the news that Caroline, his angelic ex that his mom adores is coming to stay with him. And nothing was the same after that.*

"Wait, I'm sorry, Caroline is living with your parents?" *Is this real life?* "So, your ex can move into their house, but they made you choose between them and me?" It's too much. Ben could have this great life, if he would have just walked away from me. But he didn't. I can't make sense of it. It doesn't compute. "You *chose* me. And then went running back to her? I don't understand."

Silence.

"What happened? Were you *with* her?"

"It's not like that."

"That's not a denial."

He doesn't reply. Maybe he doesn't have a good answer. Maybe he's thinking about the perfect way to explain, but my mind can't seem to piece together where we went wrong. Was it because I left for Italy? He encouraged me. This isn't fair. This is crazy.

I stare at Ben, who is kicking at the Berber carpet with the toe of his Chuck Taylor.

How did we get to the point where *I* feel like the sane one? Somehow, we ended up in this foreign place where Ben is the one standing here with wild, out-of-control eyes. It used to be *me* that was causing pain. Setting fires that couldn't be put out and walking away. I'll be honest, it was easier that way. Because just looking at him is hard enough. And forgiving? Well, that feels completely out of the question right now. I want to ask him how he did it. You know, when the situation was reversed? How was he able to stash that pain aside and still want to be with me. Because I don't think I'm that big of a person. Or strong enough. Or any of those good things that people aspire to be. I'm just a girl who was broken, who's barely had time to heal. And now, the person that claims to love me most— has just destroyed my world.

"Can you please stop doing that?" I finally break the silence. Ben obediently steadies his foot.

"I can explain it all. Just please come here," he says.

"Is this, like a payback thing? Because of Mark? We aren't past that?"

"Christ, Quinn, it's nothing like that. You're the one that kept encouraging me to go home for Christmas! There isn't anything between Caroline and me. She needed a friend—"

"Just say it. Just say that *she* needed you. That you couldn't resist running to her rescue."

His face falls, and his expression looks like I've hit the nail right on the head.

"I couldn't get ahold of you while I was gone. This is why?"

"No. Just, give me a second. Linney—"
"Oh, fuck you and your stupid pet names." I can't help but bite with venom that spews over into my words.

"Caroline was having a rough time at home," Ben says.

"Cry me a river." The 'old Quinn' is front and center.

"Quinn, I didn't go out there looking for a relationship with Caroline. She moved to a different state because she had a psychotic ex bothering her. I mean, if you think about it, you could feel a little empathy for her after what Syd went through."

"Don't even bring Sydney into this."

"You're right, I'm not. I just want you to understand. I just went out there to be a friend to her."

"I'm sure your mom loved that," I say.

"Would you just stop? Just let me explain." He pauses, and I sit back down on the sofa. He smartly takes the chair across from me, rather than next to me. "The reason Caroline had been calling before you left was because she wanted to let me know that she'd moved in with my parents. She called after you'd left and we talked and she just wasn't in a good place, Quinn. So, yeah, I flew out there to see her. *And* my family. Caroline and I talked, I spent Christmas with her and my parents, we sorted some things out, and it was good. But I thought about you the entire time, Quinn. And I love you and I missed you like crazy."

"Just not enough to answer the phone when I called, right? Why were you so late? Why did you leave me sitting at the airport without a *call*?"

"Quinn—" He reaches for me again, but I slouch away from his touch.

"Are you still in love with her?"

"Quinn, don't."

"No, that's a fair question. Answer it."

He rubs his palm along the several-day-old scruff of his cheek. He hasn't shaved in days. Four, I'd guess. Does Caroline know things like that? What Ben's stubble looks like day-to-day when he doesn't shave?

"No. I'm not in love with her. I'm in love with you. I love you. I want you. *Only you.*"

"Then why did you do this?"

"Nothing happened. I swear to you, *nothing.*"

The thing is, I mostly believe him. But he's wrong. Something did happen. He planted doubt. There was one thing that was always certain for me—and that was that I could trust him. And what he did, took that away.

"You disappeared. Wouldn't answer my calls. Didn't tell me where you were or when you'd be back. Because you were with your ex? You can't undo that. If it was so innocent, why didn't you at least tell me what was going on?"

"You're right. I screwed up. But after what happened the last time Caroline came to stay with them…You were so far away, and I was worried about what you might do."

"There it is!" I jump up from the sofa and walk to the door. "I knew that was coming. Way to throw my mistakes in my face. Thanks for giving me even a little credit, Ben."

"I didn't mean it like that, shit! I don't know what to say. I just want us to be okay."

I pull the door open.

"Well, we're not. And you need to leave."

"Quinn, can we just talk about this?" He keeps reaching for me, and I keep pulling back, each time, yanking the front door open wider and wider. He wants to touch me. Like that will be the cure for this toxic situation. But it won't. It'll only make me hurt worse.

"No. And I'll tell you why. Because I can't stand your face right now. Go stay with Carter. Run back to Caroline. I don't care. *Just leave.*"

He grabs the duffel bag he dropped by the front door on his way in and walks out. Gone. And for the second time, I've told Ben to leave. I've pushed him out of my life.

Maybe for good.
Alone.

Again.

Seventeen

QUINN

I wake up on the sofa, drool running onto my hand, and the sound of knocking on the front door pounding in my ear drums.

    I open the door just wide enough to see who it is.
    "What are you doing here?" I ask. I fidget with the end of my braid, weaving my fingers in and out of the hair.
    Ben pushes past me without bothering to answer.
    Come on in, please.
    "I know you asked me to go last night, I know," he says. His eyes are heavy. Red. Wounded.

    "I did. So, maybe you could like, respect that?" I clutch my hip, trying to look like I'm standing firm, when really I'm just trying to steady myself.

    "You've just got to understand. You've been gone for weeks. I haven't seen you. I haven't touched you...." I'm pissed. *Beyond* pissed. But the mention of his touch forces a chill down the length of my body. "And now you're back and I'm supposed to stay away?"

    His hand grazes over my shoulder lighter than a whisper. More like a memory.

"We've been over this," I say.

"We've been over a lot of things." he says. He rubs his scruffy, unshaved cheek. "We made it through last year. We can figure this out, too."

"Maybe. Or maybe we just don't work. I mean, really. Did we ever even really have a chance? Did you ever feel the way that you said you did? Or is it that once you got me, you didn't want me anymore?" I start back toward the front door and open it for him.

Take the hint, Ben. I don't have the willpower I used to. Not after everything we've been through.

"Don't say that. I can fix this. We fixed it before. We can do it again."

"I'm not sure you can. I just— I just need to figure something's out. I need some time."

"I'll give you all the time you need, baby, just please don't end this. Please."

"I don't know what I'm doing right now, Ben. I need sleep. And to try to make sense of why in the world you would up and leave to go visit your ex. I need to—"

"Marry me."

He wraps his hand around the back of my neck and pulls me in.

I'm stunned to silence.

"What are you talking about?" Is all that I can choke out.

He presses his forehead to mine. It's the closest we've been since we said good-bye at the airport last month. So much has changed since then.

He's changed.

I pull away. In all the ways it's possible to pull away from someone. I back away until I'm across the room and slouch into the windowsill, wishing it would swallow me up. That it led to some gateway to a magical place where hurt like this doesn't exist.

"Don't you understand that I trusted you? You of all people know how hard that was for me, Ben. And you killed that."

"You told me a long time ago that beautiful things never last. But I think you're wrong. I think they can. If you fight for them. If you let them change, Quinn. They can morph into something even better. If you make it work."

I do remember saying that to him. On the deck at my parents' house, the summer we first met. When I first fell in love with the boy who opened doors for me, refused to kiss me the first time without permission, and wouldn't make love to me until he was certain I loved him back.

He closes the space between us.

"Marry me," he repeats.

I push him away. "I'm not marrying you, Ben. *I'm not.* And I really think you should go."

"That was part of the reason that I was late coming home," he says. He tosses an envelope onto the coffee table and runs his hand along the back of his neck.

"Don't bullshit me, Ben. You already told me the reasons. *She* was the reason."

"You're right. I was a bastard. I know that. I know I never should have gone there in the first place. And I never should have felt tempted, but I did. And when I was, I knew I needed to get out of there and back to you. I went back to Atlanta not knowing what the fuck I was looking for, and what I figured out was that there is this part of me that can't ever be changed. And it's because you own that part."

"What does that have to do with this?" I ask, picking up the envelope and hitting my palm on one of the corners over and over again.

"Open it."

I open the envelope and pull out a small piece of paper. I have to admit, I was expecting a photo. Something dramatic that would somehow articulate how Ben feels about me and everything would be good again. Instead, it's a check. A big check. More money than either one of us thought we'd see till we were long out of school and established, respectable, real-life grown-ups.

"What is this for?" I ask. The check is made out to Ben.

"I sold a photo. Well, a pile of photos, actually."

I want to rush to him and congratulate him. I want to tell him how completely proud of him I am, and how I knew all along that this day was coming for him—sooner than later. It's what he's wanted for for so long. But I can't. I just can't.

"Before I left town, I got a call from Ron that a friend of his owns a company that wanted to acquire some of my prints. They wanted to turn them into posters to hang in restaurants and offices and stuff. I had already arranged to meet the guy that day that I came home. I had to stop by his office on my way home and sign the paperwork and pick up the check."

"I'm happy for you," I say. I mean it. Or I'm trying.

"Aren't you going to ask which pictures I sold?"

"They're all good, Ben. Which ones?"

"The photos of the sunsets that I took for you. Ones that I had had all along, that I didn't put enough value on." *The same way you didn't value us.*

He's slowly walking toward me. I back up into the kitchen. I'm running out of places to back away from him.

"I will earn your trust back. I just need you to give me some time. I can fix this, I promise." he says.

"Really? You broke my heart, Ben. Can you fix that?"

He reaches out for me again, but I put my hand up to stop him.

"Please, I can't do this right now. Please just go," I say.

~~~~~~~~~~~~~~~~~

I slide down the length of the fridge and crumple onto the checkered linoleum floor that I hate so much. I pull my knees up to my chest and bury my face in them, not caring that my hair is plastering itself to the sides of my face with tears. What happened along the way that made Ben stop caring about me? What did I do? What would drive him to pay for a plane ticket that he can barely afford, to go and see a girl he shouldn't be seeing?

Part of me aches to know every detail of what happened between them. Did they kiss? Did they do more?

The image of them kissing isn't nearly as bad as the thought of Ben, in that moment before you kiss someone. How you have to connect with someone in order to get there. Is that what he was doing with Caroline? How many moments like that did they share? How many times did he pull her into his arms—the arms that are meant to hold *me*?

The doorknob turns, and even though I just asked him to leave again, my first reaction is to hope that it's Ben. But it's not, it's Shayna.

"Hey, Carter said you were home," she says. She crosses the room and sits next to me with her legs crossed. "I missed you!" She wraps her arm around me and pulls me in.

"Are you going to pretend like you don't know what's going on?" I ask.

"Of course not, are you crazy?"

"Good. Did he stay at your place last night?"

Shayna shakes her head. "But Carter saw him on the way out, or, to be clear, Carter saw him punch his car in the parking lot and went to intervene. It's a nice car, you know?"

"Right," I say.

"I think he was going to stay up at work or something. But doesn't it make you feel a teensy-bit better to know that he isn't as perfect as you always gave him credit for? That he's way more human than any of us thought? I tell you one thing, I'm relieved. I know you must be, too."

I never thought about it like that, but it doesn't make me feel any better now that she's pointed it out. Ben was my solid. The one that I didn't have to doubt, or wonder if he was on the verge of screwing up.

We sit in silence for a few minutes. I should ask her how her Christmas was, what kind of loot she got from her folks, but I don't care about any of that, and I can't even fake it right now.

"So, what's the plan for tonight?" Shayna asks.

"Excuse me?"

"It's New Year's Eve? What are we doing? Carter and I can come over and watch movies, or something. We won't even expect you to cook. We'll spring for the take-out!"

I bury my face again and start to sob. I can't help it. Ben and I were supposed to be spending New Year's Eve together. Why are we having to spend another holiday apart?

"My parents got me a shit-ton of gift cards to restaurants in the area, so you can pick. They had it in their heads that since I don't have a job, I'm not eating well. Clearly they didn't realize what a culinary force you are—" Shayna finally takes a breath when she realizes that I'm shaking. "Wait, are you crying? I thought you were laughing, Quinn. Shit, did I make you cry?"

"I'm not laughing," I say. I look up at her, my face stained with tears and makeup and pain. "And I don't want to do anything tonight. Just leave me alone, please."

"No."

"Huh?"

"No. How long is this whole Kurt Cobain-flannel wearing-I wish it were the nineties-thing going to last? Because it's ridiculous, and *so* not you, Quinn."

I look down at my flannel shirt. I love this shirt. And I sort of hate Shayna right now.

"Shayna, just go away. You and Carter go and do something fun, I'm great here." The shirt stays, Shayna goes.

"Quinn, I'm not leaving you here alone, in this pitiful pool of tears," Shayna says.

Oh, for the love of Christ, why do I call this person my friend?

"Please. I just want to be alone right now."

"No." Shayna shakes her head at me. "We talked about this at school, how when you're hurting and you push the people away that are trying to help you, you are only dragging your pain out. Get dressed. Put on some make-up. It's the whole fake-it-till-you-make-it thing. Embrace it."

"I can't," I say, pathetically. "Not this time. I don't know how to be okay right now. I just want everyone to go away."

Shayna hoists herself off of the laminate floor, grips my shoulders and looks me dead in the eye. "You can do this,

Quinn. You can do this *without* falling apart. He fucked up, and you're entitled to feel hurt and anger and like complete and total shit. But don't let yourself become a victim of your victimhood. Don't let this destroy everything you've worked so hard for. You are not that same girl from high school. I know it. And you know it, too. Now, buck up. And put your party dress on."

Eighteen

QUINN

I don't put on a dress, but Shayna and I do compromise. I take a shower at least, and put on fresh clothes so that we can drive to pick up Chinese. It's not much, but I'll give Shayna a little credit, it does feel good to be out of the apartment where Ben's stuff is everywhere.

"Carter called while I was inside picking up the food," Shayna says, arranging herself in the passenger seat and piling the bags of takeout between us. I pull a wonton out of the bag and pop it into my mouth, even though it's really too hot to be eaten yet. It's one of my bad habits— never waiting for food to cool before I eat it. Ben is always mocking me for it— how I claim to love food so much, but I don't even wait for it to cool off so that I can actually enjoy it, rather than dancing around the kitchen, fanning my mouth and complaining about how hot it is.

"And, do we need to stop somewhere else on the way back?"

"No. Don't get pissed—"

"Too late." I interrupt. With that kind of warning, on today of all days, it's a sure bet.

"So, I guess Ben showed up at your apartment while we were out. And Carter told him he could stay with us until you guys figure stuff out."

"Traitor." And he calls himself my brother.

"Quinn, come on. Where else is he going to go?"

"You're right, it's fine. It's completely fine."

"So, he can come hang out with us for dinner and stuff, right?"

"Pushing it, Shayna."

"Think about it, at least. Do you really want him sitting in our apartment, alone, while we're all ringing in the New Year three doors away at your place?"

I reach down and turn the heat up, since it's actually pretty chilly in So Cal this week, and it almost feels like a proper winter. "We should have gone to Claim Jumper and got some chicken noodle soup," I say.

"We got wonton soup," Shayna says.

"Yeah, but I love that soup on cold nights. Oh well, I guess I can make some tomorrow."

"Sure thing. I love how you're pretending that soup is on the forefront of your mind. Not that, I don't know, you kicked your boyfriend out."

"I had to," I say, warming my hands in front of the vent until the traffic light turns green and it's my turn to go.

"No, no you didn't. Listen, I know he screwed up. I totally think it's insane that he flew all the way out there to help some broad out. And I especially think it's crazy that he didn't even bother to tell you. But boys do ridiculous, insane things all the time. He's really good to you otherwise, Quinn. And you know this."

"I don't want to talk about it right now. I'm doing what I think is best, I'm sorry if it doesn't live up to your expectations."

"That's the thing, it does. It totally lives up to everyone's expectations of the *old*-Quinn. But you aren't her."

But I am.

I glance over at Shayna and out her window, I see a man standing on the corner. He has no coat in this weather, a bag over his shoulder, and his thumb up in the air. Shayna follows my eyes over to him.

"Don't even think about it, Quinn," she says. Her voice is firm and laced with a little fear.

"It's freezing out, Shayna. He looks harmless." I steer my Prius toward the hitchhiker. As I get closer, I realize he doesn't look as benign as I first thought. But still, it *is* cold out. He must realize that I'm planning on picking him up, because he lets the large duffel he has on his back slide down on his arm and onto the ground, and he flashes a big, toothy (and fine, a little bit creepy) grin at me.

"So help me, Quinn, if you pick him up I am walking home. That means that you'll be alone with that killer."

"Judgmental much? He's not a killer. Or, it's not probable." I shrug. I pull my car over to the side of the road and hit the button to unlock the doors. Shayna reaches back behind her seat and slams the lock back down into place.

"Okay, I was wrong. You are the same Quinn. The same, reckless, dumbass Quinn. You made your point. Now take me home and then pick up all the strange men you want."

~~~~~~~~~~~~~~~~

I'm scouring my fridge for food that isn't expired since Shayna took all of the Chinese goodies to her apartment and isn't talking to me, but it appears that Ben hadn't shopped for anything but Ramen noodles and microwave dinners while I was gone. No wonder he wants me back, how could he survive on this shit?

I finally find a few ingredients that I can manipulate into a halfway decent meal when the pounding on the door begins. It's not a knock. It's so loud it makes me wonder if the person is getting a running start and careening into the door.

"Christ on a cracker, hang on!" I yell.

I open the door and for the second time today, Ben pushes past me.

"You picked up a god damned hitchhiker! Really? What the hell were you thinking, Quinn?"

I stare back at Ben. Shocked that after what he did, he's standing here. Angry at *me*.

"I didn't—"

"How about we don't do this whole routine of self-destructive bullshit just because you're hurting again."

I slam the cabinet shut and stomp toward him.

"Number one, I didn't pick him up. Number two, if you think that I'm going to risk my safety because *you* were an asshole, you greatly overestimate what you meant to me."

I watch the sharp words leave my mouth, twist through the air and pierce into him.

His body deflates.

"You're right. Happy New Year," he says, before turning and walking away.

"Ben, wait—" But it's too late, he's already stormed out.

As soon as I turn to go back into the kitchen, I hear Carter.

"He's right you know," he says, standing in the doorway. "You're lashing out because you're hurt, rather than just talking to him."

"I'm so fucking pissed, Carter," I say, tossing the package of frozen ground turkey into the microwave to defrost. "So insanely, out of my mind pissed off."

If you've never gone mad, you've never been in love.

"That may very well be. And, really, I'd probably be pretty fucking pissed off, too if I were in your shoes. But let me explain something. You being pissed doesn't give you the right to pull shit like this. Not again. And you will not put Shayna in danger because of your anger."

I start to object, but he cuts me off. "I mean it, Quinn. And beyond that, you're my sister. I don't want to see you hurt. I don't want a repeat of the last time shit hit the fan with you and Ben. No hospitals."

"Please don't," I say. The itchiness under my skin returns. I hate when I have to relive those crazy days. "I wasn't trying to put anyone in danger, I just wasn't thinking."

"And that's gotten you into trouble before, Quinnlette."

"So what am I supposed to do? I mean, relationships are hard for people that aren't totally fucked up. For me, they're just…"

"You're not fucked up, Quinn. Stop using that as an excuse to quit."

"And, so, what do I do?" I repeat the question.

"You've got two choices right now. You can walk away, or you can try harder."

Nineteen

BEN

"Orange chicken?" Shayna asks, holding up a skewered piece on the end of a pair of chopsticks.

"No thanks, not hungry," I say. Quinn's words are still breaking me inside. Like an ice pick tapping away at my heart, over and over again. I get that she's purposely trying to hurt me, and she is. I get that she's trying to push me away. We've been here before. Except this time, I don't know how to get back in. Because this time, it's all my fault.

"You sure? There's plenty, especially since that psychopath isn't going to be joining us for dinner," Shayna says with a smile that lets me know she's joking.

"She's not—"

"I know," Shayna nods. She's sitting up on the counter with her legs tucked under her. "Carter went over to talk to her. He's worried she's going to pull a second act of the last time you guys broke up."

"We aren't broken up," I say. I don't know if that's true or not, but I hope it is. I hope Quinn is just angry and we can work this out.

Shayna nods politely. Like it's all for my benefit. Like she feels sorry for me.

"Listen, I'm sorry I put you guys in an awkward position in Atlanta, with Caroline there and everything…"

"You know we didn't tell Quinn that we ran into you because we wanted to, Ben. I mean, you could've helped yourself out a little bit and actually showed up at the airport when you were supposed to."

Don't I know it. There's no way that I could ever feel like a bigger jackass than I do right now.

"So, what was the deal, anyway? What's going on with the precious ex?" Shayna is smirking.

I push my sleeves up. "I think I should talk to Quinn first. Then, you know, she can run and tell you everything."

"Probably. You know, I sort of think you're an asshole for going, though. Just so you know."

"Thanks for the honesty, Shayna."

She flips me off before going back to her dinner.

"Seriously, though. You and Quinn have been through so damn much, and you pull this?"

I shift uncomfortably. "I get it, thanks."

"I don't think you do. Because if you did, you wouldn't have gone in the first place. Were you trying to sabotage your relationship?"

"That's ridiculous."

"Is it? Because the way I see it, you've got it pretty good, Ben. You have this girlfriend that loves you. And she deserves *all* of you."

"Do you think she'll forgive me?" I ask. Shayna fancies herself a certified therapist now that she's completed a whole semester and a half of college.

"Do you regret it? I mean really? Not the part about getting caught, but do you honestly regret going?"

"No question." I'll regret getting on the damned plane for the rest of my life. "I regret not calling her more while she was gone. I regret going to Georgia. I regret it all…"

"I have a theory," Shayna says.

"Of course you do," I mumble.

"I think you pushed her away on purpose."

"Why the hell would I do that?"

"I think you pushed her away so that she'd cling to you. I think you wanted her to need you again. I mean, forget the fact that you ran across the country to be there for Caroline. Even just the little stuff. Coming home late? Sneaking out in the middle of the night to take pictures?"

"I can't sleep," I say.

"Nope, I think there's more to it. I think you have to keep moving because you're trying to mask your own issues."

"Which are?"

"That you grew up in this super strict environment, controlled by your anal-as-hell mom, and now it's basically impossible for you to figure out how to treat yourself well. So you spend your time trying to make sure everyone else is taken care of. Or, running around at night taking pictures of hobos or whatever it is that you're calling art these days."

Right now, I really think that expensive-ass USC education that Shayna's parents are footing the bill for may actually be worthwhile.

"And, because you asked, yes, I think she'll forgive your sorry ass," Shayna says just as Carter walks back in. She looks at him and smiles before adding, "If for no other reason than you're really freaking sexy, Ben."

She throws her head back as Carter shakes his at her, and I'm suddenly jealous of the casual, and secure relationship these two have. And I realize that I had that all along. That

Quinn never gave me shit about my late nights, and maybe Shayna's right. Maybe somewhere inside I wanted her to. Maybe I wanted to hear that it was hard when I was gone. Maybe after all the shit that we went through last year had settled, I didn't know how to just relax with Quinn.

~~~~~~~~~~~~~~~~

"Knock, knock," Quinn's voice wakes me up the second it penetrates my eardrums.

"Hey," I say, flinging myself up to sitting position. I alternate pulling each of my arms in front of my body, trying to stretch the best I can. Carter's couch was not made for someone my size, but I guess it's a decent punishment for what I put Quinn through.

"Sorry to wake you," she says, glancing furtively around the room.

"Carter and Shayna left early this morning, if that's what you're wondering," I say.

"Oh, okay, good. Did you sleep okay?" she asks. Her restless fingers tug at the end of her loose pony-tail. I hate that she's nervous. I hate that this is where we are. Again. Because of me. I never thought I'd be the one to bring us to this place, that I'd be the asshole that pushed us here. After all of my promises to her about how I'd take care of her, and love her, and this is where we're at.

I shrug, "I'm fine. How are you?"

"I've been better." She forces a smile, but I can tell she's not even putting in a half effort, because her jaw still looks tense when she does it.

"I know." I get up off of the couch and sit on the arm instead, making a small move to be closer to her, even if it's just another foot nearer.

"I wanted to apologize," she says, tucking a loose piece of hair behind her ear. That.That place on her neck, that's my favorite place.

"Quinn, what the hell are you apologizing for?"

"Just," she begins. She holds her hand up so I know that she's thinking about her wording and that I need to give her a minute to sort it all out. "What I said about you not meaning anything to me?"

Hearing her repeat it hurts almost as bad as the first time she said it.

"I didn't mean that. Of course, I didn't mean it."

"I know," I say. I'm shocked that she's here. Apologizing for saying what she did. And instead of making me feel better, it makes me feel even guiltier. Because Quinn has actually changed.*She's* grown, and I should have been giving her more credit all this time. I should have trusted that she would be better off knowing where I went while she was in Italy. That she wouldn't crumble. But I didn't.

"I said some pretty shitty things, too," I say, remembering the barbed words I hurled at her. "I know I'm a fuck up, Quinn, but god, I love you."

"I know," she says. And it's almost as if my ears don't believe it when she says it, because it's just too damn good to be true. Because more than anything, I just want her to believe that.

"But, I still can't do this right now. I just need some time, you know? I feel so fucking hurt and confused. And I don't understand why, if you love me, you would have run off to be with her—"

"I didn't leave to *be* with her."

"Just let me think on things, okay? I've got to go now, though. I have some things to do since I've been gone for so long…"

She tugs on her navy blue sweater. It's a simple thing, but I know it's because she's nervous and I hate that we're back at this awkward place. I have to fix this.

"Fair enough," I say. "Can I at least buy you dinner?"

"I don't know. I just feel like if we're together right now, it's going to turn into a fight, and I really don't want to fight with you, Ben. Because no matter what I said last night, I love you."

And I know that it took everything in her to open her heart enough to say those words, especially since I'd just crushed it.

"Quinn, I could apologize every day for the rest of my life. I can beg you to forgive me. *Again*. Or, I can hopefully remind you why we love each other. Can we just go back to that for a little while?"

She taps her keys against her leg and rolls her neck around. Thinking.

"It's just dinner."

Quinn blows out a long breath. "Fine. Come by the apartment tomorrow at seven. We can have dinner," she says.

I know her, and I know that right now, she's fighting that twitch of a smile in the corner of her mouth. And that in itself feels like a damn victory.

Twenty

BEN

I'm waiting at our apartment door at six-forty-two. I'm early. I had to be. I couldn't stand sitting in Carter's place a minute longer knowing that those were minutes that I could be with Quinn. But now that I'm standing here, I'm wondering if it was a mistake to show up early. Will she even let me in? Will it piss her off that I can't even follow simple directions?

I knock lightly and hold my breath.

"Hey," she says. Quinn pulls open the door, dressed casually and with one Chuck Taylor on, one in her hand. "You're early."

"I know. I could come up with some lame excuse about why, but really, I just missed you. If you want I can wait out here if you're not ready."

She shakes her head and gives me a small smile.

"No, come in. I'll let it slide this time. You still pay half the rent, after all."

I laugh, even though the statement makes me a little sad, because I know that jokes like that make her pain a little less.

She tells me to pick where we were going, but I know her well enough to know that letting me choose is basically giving me permission to pick one of her three favorite places. We end up at *El Café de la Esquina*, a little hole-in-the-wall Mexican place that's just down the street from our apartment and whose name translates into The Corner Café.

"I went by the school today," she says. "I got so many damn credits for going to Italy. I am going to graduate long before the rest of the people in my class, which I think is really crazy, right, because, I basically got the trip of a lifetime and it works out that I get to graduate early? What kind of crazy-ass dumb luck is that?" She takes a quick breath and a sip of her soda. "I'm so excited to be eating Mexican food tonight. Don't get me wrong, the food in Italy was spectacular, but I'm a little pasta'd out right now. And, I'm rambling, aren't I? Ihad this grand idea that if I just started off the evening talking, that we could bypass the awkwardness of where things are at..."

"You're great," I say. "But it doesn't have to be awkward. It's just me and you." She twists the strings of her hoodie, and I can hear the light tap the rubber soles of her Chucks under the table.

"You asked me to marry you," Quinn says, biting on her lower lip. I know what that lip tastes like. I know how it feels to nip at it. And I'd give anything to do it right now. But I can't.

"I did," I say plainly.

"That's crazy, right?"

Maybe.

"I don't know, Quinn. It felt like the thing to do."

"I don't understand how you thought that would make it any better?"

I don't know how to answer her. The truth is, I was desperate. I would have said anything to get her to understand that I love her. That my bailing to go to Georgia had nothing to do with me not loving her.

She sets her menu aside and looks me in the eyes. "What happened while you were there?"

"Can we talk about this at home?" Is it still *our* home?

Quinn gives a quick shake of her head. "I'd like to know now."

The waiter interrupts us, buying me a few minutes to figure out the best way to tell her that I kissed someone else.

But only a few very brief moments, because we order the same thing we always do, a street-food platter and duck enchiladas to share. Because that's what couples do. And I don't want to lose any of this.

"Caroline called me. Well, Caroline *had been* calling me. I didn't lie to you on Thanksgiving when I said that I didn't know why and I never called her back. I swear to you, I wasn't lying when you asked me that."

"Okay," is all that she offers.

"Anyway, I went out there and the good news is, I talked with my mom. I think things are going to be okay from now on with her. And she thanked you for the biscotti. Why didn't you tell me that you did that?"

"Why didn't you tell me you were going to Georgia to see your ex-girlfriend?" she asks. The parts that I love most about Quinn are the same parts that scare the shit out of me when I'm the one that she's angry at.

"Caroline," I say, careful not to use her nickname, because I know that it drives Quinn crazy. "She moved in with my parents because her boyfriend— or, her ex-boyfriend was accused of stalking her. He showed up at her dorm, things got really out of hand."

"Oh my god," Quinn says. "What happened?"

I pause. It's not my story to tell, but I have to.

"He attacked her. He tried to rape her. If a friend hadn't have shown up, he would have."

"Shit," she says. "Is she okay?"

"She will be. That's why she's with my folks. Her parents are trying to get it all sorted out back in Kentucky, and making sure it's safe for her to come home, you know?"

"So, that's it? You just went out there to help her get settled and hung out and stuff?"

I have to tell her. I can't tell her. I have to tell her.

I watch Quinn tense up. "What is it, Ben?"

I shift in my chair and feel like a coward I am. Quinn knows there's more.

"She tried to convince me to stay. With her."

"What?" she says through clenched teeth.

"Caroline is lonely, and scared, and for her, I'm this safety net."

"No, no you're not. You aren't in a relationship with *Caroline*, Ben. Did you forget that while you were there? Settle back into old habits, or what?"

"I didn't reciprocate, I swear to you, baby—"

"What? Didn't reciprocate? Never mind, I have to go. I have to leave." Quinn slams her palms down onto the table as she stands up.

"Quinn, come on, it's not what you think."

But she grabs her purse off of the back of her chair and hauls ass out the door. Away from me.

I easily catch up with her in the parking lot where she's standing there, shaking with anger. Because of me.

"Quinn—"

"I just want to go home," she says.

"Okay, get in the car. I'll drive you."

"No thanks, I'll walk. It's not far."

"I don't feel safe with you out here alone at night, Quinn. Let me drive you home."

Quinn spins on her heals and glares at me.

"Ben, unlike Caroline, *I* don't feel safe with you." Her words are the daggers she intends them to be.

Twenty-one

QUINN

"Fine, take my car then, I'll walk. I don't want you out here alone at night." Ben tosses me the keys to his car, the same one that I rode in the very first day I met him and then he turns to start the walk home. I'm not made of stone. It does occurs to me that it's a crappy thing to do, to let him walk away while I drive his car home. But my anger doesn't let me stop it from happening.

I'm adjusting the driver's seat to accommodate my short-as-hell legs when the passenger door opens and Ben slides in.

"What are you doing?" I ask. I reach for the door handle to get out. The apartment really isn't that far.

"Don't leave. Please. Don't run away. Not this time."

It's infuriating that he's acting like I have the choice to do anything *but* run. I thought I was ready to hear it all, but I'm not. When he started talking about Caroline wanting him back, all of my fears slammed into me at once. How I've never been able to live up to the angelic Caroline. How she still wanted him, and maybe always will. How can I compete with perfection like her?How maybe Ben would be better off choosing her instead. And I'm scared that when he tells me what happened, that it may break me. That this shell with crumble and the old Quinn will step out of it. Angry and damaged and empty inside.

"I fucked up, Quinn. I know that I did. But you asked what happened. I didn't want to do this here, but you're the one that insisted. And you know what? I want you to know. I want it all out in the open, Quinn.Because I'm losing you without you even knowing. I need to at least *try* to make you understand."

I sit there, silent. The familiar smell of Ben's cologne is all around me. I think about how many times I kissed him goodnight in this car. How many times he dropped me back off at my parents' house, when all I wanted to do was curl up in this space and stay with him. Because I felt safe and loved like I never had before. I ache to feel that right now.

"I talked to my mom about you," he says, tracing a circle on the knee of his jeans with his fingertip. I want to make some snarky ass remark about how I'm sure that went over well, but I don't. "I think she's coming around. It'll be slow, I don't want to lie and say things are perfect, but she knows you're it for me. And you *are,* Quinn. You're it. You always have been." He looks up from his pants and tries to catch my eye, but I don't give in.

"Things with Caroline...I never meant for it to go that far. I don't know what I thought was going to happen. I just wanted to be there for her as a friend, I swear to you, that's all I went there for. But once I got there and I saw how broken down she was, it was like, something else took over. This need to protect her. She's been in my life for a long time, Quinn, I couldn't just turn my back on her."

"I know that," I say. And, I guess I partly do. Because I've always sort of known that that part of Ben existed. The good-guy who wants to take care of people. It's just been me that he wanted to take care of before. How can I accept that he feels the same about someone else, too? And flying across the country to see his ex without telling me. "But you could have gone about it a different way. You could have been there for her over the phone. Or, you could have talked to me before you left."

"You're right. I'm realizing how right you are about so many things lately. I finally get that Caroline wanted me back all along. It wasn't something you made up, it was real. She's hurting, and scared, but this was something more. I'm so sorry I never took it seriously, if I had, I never would have gone."

I normally feel victorious when people tell me that I'm right, but this time, there's nothing to cheer about.

"And so that it's all out on the line…she kissed me," he says.

I feel an electric current of anger at Caroline and sadness that Ben has kissed someone else, and guilt that I did so much worse last year course through me.

"I don't need to hear this," I say. I'm shaking. Shaking like the weak person I claim not to be anymore.

"Yes, you do. She kissed me, but I didn't kiss her back, Quinn, I couldn't. I told her to go. And I'm pretty sure that she hates me right now, but that's okay, because I love you, Quinn. *Only you.* And I'm sorry that my needing to be needed ruined things. I had no idea how fucked up I was until I made the mistake of going home. But trust me, it's been clear since then." I listen to Ben fumble over his words. I want to make it easier for him, but I don't know what to say. He's right, he did this.

"I wanted you to need me, and when you didn't—"

"I did need you, Ben. That's the point. I've always needed you. I needed you to be solid. To be constant. And this…what you did…"

I watch the time change on the digital clock on the dash, and can't help wondering, what if this is the last time that we sit in the car together. 8:21. Will the time always stick out in my mind like everything else with Ben? Every time I woke up with him carrying me to bed after I'd fallen asleep on the couch. Every time I came home from school, frustrated and tired and he was there to tell me a story to make it better? Every time I hung up the phone with my mom, and felt deflated and pessimistic at the entire world, and how he'd swipe the tears from under my eyes before they fell?

"You didn't kiss her back?" I ask. It doesn't matter, because in my mind they had a romp in the middle of his mother's precious container room, even though I know that's highly unlikely.

"I didn't. I swear. But…When she kissed me…I was in the shower."

"Oh for fuck's sake," I say.

"I just want everything out in the open, baby. I don't want shit coming out later on…if there is a later on."

"So you were late because you were showering with Caroline?"

"No. Never. I swear. She came into the bathroom while I was showering."

Ever heard of locks, asshole?

"I was late because she was hysterical after I shot her down and I couldn't leave her like that at my parents' house, Quinn. I had to take a later flight and then my connection was delayed, and it was like the entire fucking universe was conspiring against me getting home to you."

"Is that all? That's the whole story?"

"Yes."

"I need to go then. I need you to go. I can't process this right now."

"Okay," he says. He gets out of the car, shuts the door and I let him walk away.

I slam the pot down onto the stove, turn the flame on high and toss a pack of ground beef into the skillet for tacos. I missed out on Mexican food last night. I'm going to eat it for breakfast. I slept like shit knowing Ben was down the hall at Carter and Shayna's house. I got up at an ungodly hour expecting Shayna to be here bright and early with some scoop about how he is, but she wasn't.

The front door swings open just as I'm grating a massive pile of cheddar cheese.

"Do you ever knock?" I ask.

Ben shrugs. "Sorry, habit."

"Whatever. Your car keys are on the table by the door if that's what you're looking for."

"I'm glad you're okay," he says.

"Am I?" I feel angry. I feel hurt. I feel all the things that are the *opposite* of okay.

"You're home. You're safe."

"Flour or corn?" I ask, holding up two packages of tortillas.

"Quinn, you don't have to cook for me."

"You know that cooking is therapeutic for me. I'm doing this for *myself*, not you."

Ben nods and shoves his hands into his pockets. "Good. And corn, please."

Twenty-two

BEN

I sit on a barstool and silently watch her cook. Watching her move around the kitchen in those skimpy-ass shorts and a t-shirt that she's practically swimming in is one of the most beautiful things I've ever seen. Every movement is fluid and precise. And even though she's angry at me, I can tell that cooking is filling her with a form of peace that nothing else could offer her. The first day I met Quinn, she cooked for me. I remember leaning back in that barstool at her parents' house feeling nervous as hell because I'd never met a girl like this. Now, I'm sitting here scared that I'll have to let her go. I'd do anything to not have to face that reality.

I don't say a word, because I don't want to ruin the moment, but also because I know that Quinn didn't invite me, and even though she hasn't kicked me out yet, I know she needs quiet.

She sets a plate down in front of me. "There's fresh guacamole in the fridge. I'm going to change."

And on a normal day, I'd follow her into the bedroom and try to make her late for school, but today, I just sit and chew my food slowly, trying to drag my visit out as long as possible.

Quinn reappears a few minutes later with wet hair and wearing her typical jeans, sweatshirt and flip flops.

"Any good?" she asks.

"Delicious. I've missed your cooking."

"I bet. The cabinets were pretty bare when I first got home. Course, you weren't here…"

She doesn't say it as a dig, and I think that makes it that much worse.

She fixes a plate and sits across from me, and all I can concentrate on is the smell of her shampoo that lingers in her wet hair, and how many times I've climbed into the shower and washed it for her. Or tried to. Usually we'd both just end up covered in suds and couldn't keep our hands off of each other.

"Last night—"she says.

I swallow the last bite of food and wipe my mouth with a paper towel.

"I'm sorry," I say.

"I understand what you were saying about my not needing you," she says. "I mean, I do need you. I meant that. I always have. It's just in a different way. Before, I felt like I needed you to rescue me from my insane home life…and maybe from myself."

And I remember all of those nights that she'd shown up on my doorstep, wounded and lonely and needing me to hold her. Until she didn't.

"And now…Now I need you to be there when I wake up in the morning," she says.

"I want that. More than anything."

"I also need you to be there in the middle of the night."

I'm scared as hell right now that I'm losing the only person I've ever really given a damn about. That I tore what we had to shreds and that she's never going to forgive me. What can I say to make that not happen? What can I do?

"I understand," is all I say.

"I've got to get going. I have class.First day back."

She gives a small nod, then wipes her hands and gets up from her chair.

I catch her forearm as she passes me. "I do love you, Quinn. Even if I fucked it all up."

"I know. Just let me have some time."

"Okay," I say, hoping I'm strong enough to give it to her. I walk to the door with her, because I'm not sure she wants me here while she's gone. I'm not sure it's my home anymore.

"Thanks for breakfast," I say.

"Sure." She twists her hair back into a loose bun on top of her head and secures it with a chopstick that she swiped off the counter. "What are your plans this week?"

"To win you back. That's it. That's my plan.Every day."

Twenty-three

BEN

"Not the black one," Shayna says, crinkling her nose. "Go with the gray cardigan."

I sigh. Quinn should be the one helping me pick out clothes for this event.

It's not like I haven't seen her, because I have— almost every day. She comes by Carter's place, or the three of us go over to the apartment that still contains most of my stuff, but I haven't had a real conversation with her in weeks.

"What color tie?" I ask Shayna.

"Go with purple," she says. "It's Quinn's favorite color."

"Okay," I say. I wish Quinn would be there to see it. I grab the purple one of the tangled bunch that I pulled out of one of my boxes from our apartment. My mom would not approve of this organization. And that makes me smile.

"Have you invited her, bro?" Carter asks, hopping down off of the counter top.

"Nah," I say. It crossed my mind. I'm going to an unveiling of the line of posters that I sold my photos for tonight. There's no one that I'd rather have there, that should be there, more than Quinn. She inspired the pictures that have changed my life. But I'd trade every cent to have her back. "I didn't want her to feel obligated to go or anything."

"Don't be stupid, just invite her. It's not like she has anything going on," Shayna says.

"Shay—" Carter warns. "Stay out of it."

Shayna rolls her eyes. "Whatever. You should be more involved in it, Carter," she says.

"Hell no, my sister can handle her own business," he says.

That she can.

"Well, if she doesn't start handling it, Ben here will be living with us forever," Shayna says.

I had considered it, though no one has said anything. If Quinn doesn't let me back into her life, what then? Where do I go? I finally have a little money to my name, I could go get a place around here, but man, packing up my stuff and bringing it to a place that doesn't have Quinn sounds really freaking depressing.

"Don't listen to her, man, you can stay as long as you want."

"I'm kidding, Ben," Shayna assures me.

And once again I feel pitied, and I don't deserve to.

"I can't," I say. "I told her I'd give her some time." And I have to. It's the only choice I have.

"If you ask me, and you didn't, I think you should talk to her. At least invite her," Carter says.

I want to. But I can't.

"I'll think about it," I say, even though I don't mean it. If I push Quinn, I could lose her forever. I can't risk it just because I'm impatient. No way.

"What time do we need to be there?" Shayna asks.

"It starts at seven, but you guys, don't feel like you have to—"

"Ben, please. We're going. Who else is going to be there to show up for you?"

I called my mom and told her about it. She cried. In a good way. I sort of feel like maybe I've proved that this is a real thing to her now that I've sold a piece of work. I had to ask her about Linney. I had to. She's gone back to Kentucky, though she's staying at her parents' house, not her dorm. She's got a restraining order against the douche that fucked up her life, and the DA has picked up charges against him. I've learned that I can care about Linney, and that's okay, but there have to be some boundaries. I want her to be happy, but the only person I need in my life is Quinn.

Shayna leaves the room to change for the event.

Carter comes to stand next to me by the bar. "Look, you've always been good to my sister, that's why I'm pulling for you guys to work it out. And I like you, dude, I do. I'm all for second chances. But she's my sister. Fuck with her again—"

"I know. Trust me. I know," I say. "If somehow I'm able to get her back, I'll never fuck it up."

Carter nods. "Good luck, man."

Twenty-four

QUINN

"Any more pictures?" Teresa asks.

"No, I think that's it," I say. I tuck the photos that I finally had developed into my server's apron. "But I do have some balsamic vinegar that I bought there. I'll bring you a bottle tomorrow. It's life changing stuff." I smile at Teresa's enthusiasm. She's been chomping at the bit to hear every story and see every photo since I got back to LA. Every afternoon when I come in from school, she's waiting to grill me for more details. There are worse things than reliving that experience, though.

I miss Italy, and Amalea, but it's good to be settling back into a normal routine...even if it's been a new one. Adjusting to a day-to-day life without Ben has been strange. I'm not even angry at him anymore. I sort of understand why he went to help Caroline. But understanding doesn't erase the betrayal I feel that he didn't tell me. I see him every day. He's living three doors away with Carter, it's hard not to. And late at night, I sometimes walk downstairs to the parking lot to see if his car is there, hoping to 'accidently' run into him coming in from taking pictures because, as much as I told him that I need space, I miss him something fierce.

"Your friend is here," Teresa says, pointing over my shoulder. My stomach dances with nervous butterflies, expecting to see Ben's face when I turn around. But it isn't. Shayna is over by the hostess stand, waving like an idiot.

"Hey, what are you doing here?" I walk over and ask. "Everything okay?" Shayna has only been to the restaurant twice, and she was forced. This level of dining isn't up to her hoity standards, apparently.

"Yeah, yeah, everything's fine. Are you off?"

I glance at my watch. "In ten minutes, why?"

"Rad, I have a change of clothes for you in my car, I'm going to bring it in and you can change in the bathroom. We're kind of pressed for time, so we'll just pretend that your hair doesn't look like that," she says.

"Where are we going?" I ask, ignoring the insult.

"It's a surprise!" Shayna squeaks.

"I hate surprises," I deadpan.

"I know! That's what makes it even funner for me!"

I hate Shayna. Not really, but sometimes I want to.

"Fine." It beats spending the night in the apartment alone. It's odd that Ben somehow ended up with my only friend and my brother. I probably should have thought that plan through better when I asked him to be the one to leave.

I clock out, change into the black dress and heels that Shayna has packed for me and meet her out in her car.

"So, where are we going?" I ask, tugging on the hem of the dress.

"You'll see." Shayna says. She's dressed up. In a colorful maxi dress full of peridot, cobalt, and violet that sort of reminds me of the aurora borealis.

"Shay, come on. If I have to wear this, I want to know what's going on."

"Ugh, oh fine. Baby. We're going to the unveiling of Ben's poster-thing."

"What? That's tonight? Why didn't he tell me?"

"Uh, because you told him to leave you alone for a while. Anyway, yeah, they're having a showing of the line of all of the ones they acquired at some gallery, downtown. Who knew they made fine-art posters? Talk about a niche market. Anyway, surprise!"

The gallery is packed. People are filing in from three different entrances. Who knew that posters drew such a big crowd? I feel insanely out of my element.

"Drink?" A waiter passes by and offers me a glass of champagne.

"No thank you," I say. This is awfully hoity.

I should hate Shayna for springing this on me, but I don't. Because I wouldn't want to miss this for anything—seeing Ben in his moment, being recognized for his amazing talent is worth the discomfort of a borrowed wool dress and heels that are a half-size too small.

There's a row of easels displaying the various posters that they've made from the photos that they bought. Ben's poster is second to last. And just like he said, it contains each of the shots of the sunsets he took for me. They're lined up in rows and he's signed the bottom of the poster. Each print will have his signature. It's incredible.

I close my eyes and remember the look on his face when he gave me that book. We were so far away from okay at that point, but he knew that things would be okay someday. So he took those photos every day that we were apart, and now they're here, for everyone to enjoy.

I scan the room until I find Ben. He's across the room, but still easy to find. He's in jeans, a gray cardigan and a tie. I love seeing him in his own casual version of dressy. It was one of the first things I ever noticed about him. He looks overwhelmed in the large crowd, even though he's taller than the majority of it. He catches my eye and gives me a small, grateful smile. The same smile I've seen so many times. And it dawns on me that he didn't change at all. That the same Ben is still standing right there. That he screwed up, because he's human. He'd been my version of perfect for so long, I never considered that there'd be a time when he'd let me down, but it had to happen eventually, because nothing in life is that perfect. And that's okay. Ben screwing up gave me the opportunity to prove that I could go through something and not fall apart.

Ben put everything on the line to be with me, even after my big fuck-up. He never stopped loving me, he just got confused, and maybe a little broken. And I guess everyone is allowed a second chance.

There is nothing standing in the way of Ben and me being happy but me. I'm not in a situation like Amalea where I have these horrible circumstances keeping me from the man I love. He's right there.

He's *always* been right there.

Twenty-five

QUINN

"Thanks for bringing me home," I say. I'm standing in the doorway to our apartment. I could have had Ben bring me back to my car. I could have. But to be honest, I wasn't ready to say good-bye to him at the gallery. Tonight of all nights, I just couldn't let him go.

"No problem. Thanks for showing up tonight. I really can't imagine doing that without you being there."

I stare back at him. I don't know what to say to make things okay right now. All I know is that I don't want it to be ten years from now, and have me sitting there wondering why I stayed angry, or hurt, or feeling guilty for so long without Ben. I don't want to end up like Amalea, torturing myself over what could have been.

"Just let me know when you want to go get your car tomorrow, I can take you," Ben says. "Thanks," I say. *Stupid girl.*

"I love you," he says. Before I can open my mouth to say it back, he continues. "I used to think I loved you because of the way you made me feel that first day we spent together in

Savannah. But I don't. I love you for the way you crinkle your nose when someone annoys the shit out of you, and you're trying so damn hard to bite your tongue. I love you for never burning food. I love you for calling me out on my shit, and reminding me every day why I'm so damn lucky to call you mine. I love you for making my life whole."

He gives me a small, warm smile, like he's thinking the same thing that I am. That he doesn't want this night to end yet.

"I think you should stay," I say. I take the last few steps toward him.Close enough to see the stubble on his cheeks and neck. Close enough to smell the fresh, soapy scent that *is* Ben. Close enough to fall in love with him again.

"Are you sure?" Ben tiltshis head to the side like he's not sure he's heard me right.

I nod and link my arms around him, pressing myself into him. I've been aching for his touch for weeks.He doesn't let me go, picking me up and carrying me into our apartment and the door shut behind us.

"I don't think I'll ever let you go again," he says.

"Don't," I say.

He carries me to the couch.

"I love you, Ben," I say. I know he's going to say it, and I want to be the one to say it first this time. The words tumble out easily, just like they have a thousand times before, but I need him to know it. To understand that it's real. That it's forever.

I lace my arms around the back of his neck and he pulls me in, his lips warm on my ear. "I love you, too."

His dark eyes are hazy with that unmistakable look he gives me when he wants me. And it feels amazing to be wanted.

"I never want to be away from you again," he says. His words are a hot rush of breath on my neck, and the only words that need to be said.He lays back on the sofa and pulls me onto his lap. I tilt my hips up against him and I can feel that he's instantly hard.

There's not a minute of fumbling hesitation before we're both tugging on each other's clothes. I works on his sloppily knotted tie. He slides the zipper of the dress down my back, then runs his hands along the now bare skin. He slips them under the straps and lets them fall off of my shoulders.

We're stripped bare. Everything out in the open. Everything lost and then found again. Every ounce of hurt and guilt replaced by the love that we've fought so hard for.

And for a moment, it feels like too much. Too much at stake again. I start to move to cover myself with my arms.

"Don't," he says, pulling them away from my chest. "You're so beautiful."

His lips are on my throat, and his hands slip under the black lace of my bra, cupping my breasts, tugging on my nipples. I can't kiss him hard enough.

Ben pulls back for a second so that I can help him tug his shirt off over his head so that we both are skin on skin, and then his mouth is on me again. He pushes the scrap of lace of my panties out of the way and lets his fingers slide inside me.

"Ben," I gasp. I've missed his touch more than I thought. I fist my hands in his hair and tug on it. His capable hands get to work until the room is spinning and I can't string a coherent thought together.

"I need you," I say. The three words come out like a beg.

He pulls away long enough to grab a condom and my breath is rushing out so fast and uneven, it's hard to know if I'm exploding into a million pieces because I'm crashing towards terror or bliss.

I lay back onto the sofa as Ben steadies himself above me, not letting any of his weight push onto me. But I want him to. I pull him down toward me and he locks eyes with me again.

"I love you, baby," he says. And then he's inside of me, and we are in that perfect rhythm that ours. But it's not close enough this time. I wrap my legs around his waist. I pull him in closer. I rise up to meet him. It's scratching and tugging and kissing until I taste tin. It's a desperate attempt to make up for lost time and to show each other how much we've been missing each other.

"You feel so damn amazing," Ben says. He pulls me onto his lap again and takes one of my nipples in his mouth, sending me over the edge.

I try to match his breathing to steady my own as he slides in and out of me. And it's the perfect antidote because we're in this together. Everything. Together.

"I missed, you," I say, falling limp against his chest. Relaxed. Loved. Home.

And later, falling asleep on Ben, with his hands tangled in my hair—in our bed— in this home that we've made together, I know that this reunion was more than worth the wait.

EPILOUGE

"Is this one of those typical female, 'I don't know what to wear to the party' things?" Ben says, surveying the pile of dresses I've laid out across our bed.

"No, it's an '*I don't know what to wear to watch my brother get engaged kind of thing,*'" I say. "I mean, who knows what he's got planned, right? He could have given us more of a heads up. Details, Carter, details are helpful," I mumble.

"Easy there, tiger, it's not a big deal. I'm sure it's going to be low-key."

"I just can't believe it's happening so fast, I mean, I thought Syd would be the first person I knew to run off and get married."

"Well, they aren't technically married yet. She may not even say yes," Ben jokes.

"Oh, she'll definitely say yes." I kick off the black heels I'd been wearing around the room while I try on dresses. "Holy shit, how did it not dawn on me before that Shayna is going to be my *sister*." I say the last word like it's a dirty word.

"She's not half-bad, admit it."

"Never." I joke. "It's at the Four Seasons, for Christ's sake. Who is Carter trying to impress?"

"Shayna's family," Ben chuckles.

"True. " I agree. I toss aside the red dress that is definitely out of the running. "I just can't decide."

"Anything you wear will be fine."

I hold up the navy dress that I bought in Italy and stare in the mirror, as Ben walks up behind me, wrapping his arms around my waist and burying his face in the crook of my neck.

"You smell good," I tell him.

He takes the dress from my hands and tosses it back onto the bed.

"Tell you what," he says, rubbing his calloused hand across my chest, "You try them on, and I'll take the ones I don't like off of you."

I turn to face him and he pushes my robe off of my shoulders. "You know what else is typical of parties? Being fashionably late," Ben growls, pulling me onto the bed with him.

"Wait, wait, wait!" I squirm away from him. "We can't do this right now. We cannot be late to this party."

"Yes we can," he says.

"No! My parents are going to be there, too, and I'm not going to give them the satisfaction of showing up late and looking like the asshole of the family."

"Quinn, who cares what they think?"

I consider this for a minute, while I nip at his ear and neck. I'm not even remotely helping the situation, I know.

"Okay, okay," Ben shrugs me off. "Could we be late for this?"

He reaches inside his pocket and pulls out a box.

A box that looks like it contains jewelry.

A jewelry box that looks like it contains a *ring*.

"Ben, we can't do this. Not today. This is my brother's day and…" I love Ben. I do. I love him with every single cell inside my body. I want him forever. But we aren't nearly ready for this.

"Shhh…" he says. He covers my lips with his index finger. "It's okay. It's not what you think."

"Huh?" I ask. I didn't want it to be, but the fact that I *assumed* that *it* was an engagement ring leaves me a little embarrassed and flustered. I start picking at the polish on my right hand, but Ben takes my hand to stop me.

"You just painted them, Quinn. Why are you nervous? It's just me."

He hands me the box and I rub my hand across the smooth, velvet exterior. Ben's right, I shouldn't have been picking at my nails. The silver polish I'd just applied an hour ago is now missing from my middle finger. I trace the gold band around the middle where the box will croak open, but I'm too nervous to do it.

"I just, I don't want to screw anything up. I want to say the right thing and…"

"Just open it."

I take a deep breath and pry the tiny box open.

Inside, as Ben promised, is not a ring.

It's a scrap of white paper, tucked in the crease of the box where a ring would normally go. Ben's slanty chicken scratch is pressed deep into the paper because he always presses too hard when he's concentrating.

I promise.

"What's this?" I ask.

Ben smiles and pushes the hair back out of my face.

"I can't promise that I'll ever be able to give you the big house, or the best Damascus knives or that I'll ever be able to tell the difference between a Coeur à la Crème mold and a soufflé dish. I can't promise that I'll never piss you off, or that I'll never let you down again. I can't promise to always say the right things, or even to pretend that you always say the right things. But I can promise, and I *do* promise, that I'll wake up every single day and try like hell. I promise you that I'll give you everything in me."

The tiny hairs on the back of my neck perk up in the best way, like when a cool breeze catches you on a miserably hot Southern day, and I know, holding that box with Ben's promise that it was all worth it. All of it. Every miss-step, every person who tried to threaten the love that we have, every harsh word and round of makeup sex. Every single touch in the middle of the night, every single thing that went wrong or right brought us to this exact place.

To this lesson.

I finally understand that life isn't about holding all of the pieces neatly together. Life is about picking up the pieces. And love is about finding a way to make those pieces fit together, even if they're all jaggedy and mismatched. And that's what brought Ben and I to this moment— to this mad, crazy love.

To this *promise*.

That beautiful things can last, if you let them bend and change with you.

Acknowledgments

Hugethanks go out to so many people:

First, my husband Chris, thanks for running the show while I write. I literally could not do it without you. Any of it. Love you.

My kids! I love you, Hailey, Liam, Finnian & Britta. I don't spend as much time with you as I'd like, but I promise, it's all *for* you. I'm so honored to be your mom.

To Liz Reinhardt, to call you my best friend seems inadequate, because you're more like my hetero-life-mate. Thanks for keeping me on track when I got sidetracked and just wanted to peruse where to order sfogliatelle online. Thanks for annihilating my apostrophes, and schooling me on the oxford comma repeatedly. I owe you A's weight in Grappa. *In Italy.* I love you.

To Jolene Perry, who plucked Grounding Quinn out of obscurity back in 2011, when I was a very newly self-published author (before self-publishing was acceptable) and became my (and Quinn and Ben's) biggest cheerleader, writing partner, fashion consultant, and friend. *Thank you.*

To readers like Fred LeBaron, Kelly Moorhouse, and Carly Noonan, who not only 'got' Quinn, but embraced her from the start. Thank you for your enthusiasm and willingness to see past her tough outer-shell and love her despite her flaws. I adore you all to pieces!

Thanks to my rock star cover artist, Sarah Hansen who has also become a dear friend and my book soul mate.

To Ron Pope, for the title inspiration, and for writing beautiful music and sharing your amazing gift. And special thanks to Blair for making things happen!

Big shout out to my agents, Jane Dystel and especially to the lovely Lauren Abramo, both of Dystel and Goderich, who put up with my inane questions and are some of the smartest people I know! So lucky to have you in my corner!

Thanks to our favorite traveling mates, Phil, Judy, Chris, Ian, Skye, Mark, Susan and Lu-Lu, and, of course, our tour guide Davide, for leaving Chris and I with such incredible memories of Italy that I had to include it in a book.

Last and never least, thank you to the ladies of FP. My cohorts, colleagues, and friends that I am so honored to call such. Thanks for being there every single day to inspire, make me laugh, tell me

I'm ridiculous, offer a shoulder, build me up— but always keeping me grounded and keeping things real.

About the Author

Steph Campbell grew up in Southern California, but now calls Southwest Louisiana home. She has one husband, four children and a serious nail polish obsession.

Other Novels by Steph are:

DELICATE (YA)

GROUNDING QUINN (Mature YA)

MY HEART FOR YOURS (co-written with Jolene Perry) New Adult Romance

LENGTHS (co-written with Liz Reinhardt) New Adult Romance

A TOAST TO THE GOOD TIMES (co-written with Liz Reinhardt)New Adult Romance

Steph blogs at stephcampbell.blogspot.com, stop by and say hello!

www.facebook.com/authorstephcampbell

@stephcampbell_

Made in the USA
Lexington, KY
25 March 2013